'No.' He spoke softly r... ...Don't you see, Jules?' The words were being forced out. He shouldn't be saying them. But he could no more *not* say them than take in another breath. 'It's not that I *have* to protect you so much. It's that I *want* to. Too much.'

Slowly, her gaze lifted. Caught his and held it.

Mac's hands fisted by his sides as a defence against the urge to reach out and pull her into his arms. He tried to smile, but could only manage a brief, one-sided twist of his mouth. 'It's a bit of a problem,' he confessed. 'It has been ever since that… kiss.'

THE BABY GIFT

A gift so special it's priceless

WISHING FOR A MIRACLE

Julia Bennett thinks she's come to terms with not being able to have a child of her own. But then she meets Mac, and would love for them to have a little family. But Mac knows that with Julia in it his life is complete…anything else is a blessing…

*'We can make all our dreams come true
if we do it together.'
Julia's smile wobbled. 'You know what?'
'What?'
'I actually believe that.'*

THE MARRY-ME WISH

Anne Bennett has been a mother already. She gave up her own childhood when her parents died and she had to bring up her baby sister Julia. Whilst she wouldn't change that for the world, she's finally living her own life. A talented surgeon, she's at the top of her game— but she knows there is one last, precious thing she can do for her sister…

*When they came back from their honeymoon
Anne had a gift waiting for them. A promise.
'I want to be a surrogate mother for you,' she said.*

But how will Anne's gorgeous ex-fiancé cope when he sees her pregnant?

**This month read the stories of both Bennett girls by favourite author Alison Roberts.
You'll laugh, cry, and be swept away on a heart-warming journey as both these young women find their happy-ever-after, whilst two sweet little bundles of joy steal your heart!**

WISHING FOR A MIRACLE

BY
ALISON ROBERTS

MILLS & BOON®

First published in Great Britain 2010
Large Print edition 2011
Harlequin Mills & Boon Limited,
Eton House, 18-24 Paradise Road,
Richmond, Surrey TW9 1SR

© Alison Roberts 2010

ISBN: 978 0 263 21716 2

Harlequin Mills & Boon policy is to use papers that are
natural, renewable and recyclable products and made
from wood grown in sustainable forests. The logging and
manufacturing process conform to the legal environmental
regulations of the country of origin.

Printed and bound in Great Britain
by CPI Antony Rowe, Chippenham, Wiltshire

Dear Reader

I'm not lucky enough to have a sister, but I do have an amazing daughter and many truly wonderful friends, so I'm well aware of what an astonishingly powerful thing the bond between women can be.

Friends, mothers and daughters…sisters. I started thinking about the kind of bond that might be created if it encompassed all of these possibilities. Could it be enough to overcome obstacles that seem impossible?

Neither Julia nor Anne Bennett envisages a future that involves children. Their reasons might be different, but the effect their convictions have on their relationships has the potential to be disastrous.

But Jules and Annie are more than simply sisters, and their bond is such that they will go to extraordinary lengths to help each other.

As far, even, as carrying a child for the one who can't.

That kind of bond is amazing all on its own, but I wanted to give these sisters even more. Men who love them for exactly who they are and futures that will allow all their dreams to come true.

Cherish the women in your life. The bond is magic.

With love

Alison

Alison Roberts lives in Christchurch, New Zealand. She began her working career as a primary school teacher, but now juggles available working hours between writing and active duty as an ambulance officer. Throwing in a large dose of parenting, housework, gardening and pet-minding keeps life busy, and teenage daughter Becky is responsible for an increasing number of days spent on equestrian pursuits. Finding time for everything can be a challenge, but the rewards make the effort more than worthwhile.

Recent titles by the same author:

NURSE, NANNY...BRIDE!
HOT-SHOT SURGEON, CINDERELLA BRIDE
THE ITALIAN SURGEON'S CHRISTMAS MIRACLE

CHAPTER ONE

THE train lay like a jagged open wound across the soft, misty Scottish landscape.

One carriage was still on the bridge, anchored by the tangled metal of broken overhead beams. The engine and two more carriages were in the gully, some thirty metres below, partially submerged by the small but fast-moving river. Another hung, suspended somehow by the mess of twisted steel on the bridge, a gigantic pendant that encased goodness knew how much human misery.

'Target sighted.'

The quiet statement from the man staring down from beside the helicopter pilot was superfluous except that the inflection on the second word said it all. This wasn't the usual kind of target they set out to locate. This was, quite probably, a once-in-a-career, major, multi-casualty incident.

This was…huge.

Julia's determined intake of breath was clearly communicated via the equipment built into their helmets.

'How 'bout that, Jules?' The rich, male voice of her partner filled her earphones again. 'Not something you'd see every day back home, is it?'

She wouldn't want to either but it was exactly what she'd come to the other side of the world in search of, wasn't it? In a small country like New Zealand, the chance to be involved with a rescue mission of this size was highly unlikely. Working in the UK was all about getting the experience in case it did happen. Having the opportunities to hone the skills she knew she had.

She hadn't anticipated this sudden rush of adrenaline, however. A sinking, almost sick-making dive occurring in her belly. Julia swallowed hard.

'It's what I signed up for,' she said. 'Bring it on!'

'Hold your horses, lassie.' It had been nearly

three months since Julia had joined this new specialist emergency response team and the pilot, Joe, had learned to hide his vague incredulity that such a slender, feminine creature could be so keen to hurl herself into danger but there was still the suggestion in his tone that she had to be at least halfway crazy. 'There's a Medivac chopper taking off. We haven't got clearance to land yet.'

'And then we'll have to check in with Scene Command,' her partner reminded her. 'See where we're needed first.' A hint of tolerance born of understanding crept into his voice. 'Joe's right. Hold those horses.'

The tolerance had been hard won but Alan MacCulloch was used to her enthusiasm by now. Appreciated it, even, now that he knew she wasn't about to rush headlong into a scene and put them both in danger, and this had become a tradition. Julia was the feisty one, ready to leap in and do whatever needed to be done. Mac was the calm one. They both looked but Mac got to give the word before either of them leapt. It was one of the many things they had found that made them able to work so well together. Had forged them into a tight team in a surprisingly short space of time.

The scene commander wasted no time in briefing them. Dealing with the carriages that had crashed to ground level was under control.

'Carriage 3...' The scene commander looked up. 'Still an unknown quantity for victim numbers and status. One bloke got the door open near the top and managed to climb out. He fell.'

Julia exchanged a glance with Mac. They both knew how unlikely it was that someone would have survived such a fall. The dangers inherent in this rescue were becoming very clear.

'Someone else was spotted signalling for help,' the scene commander continued. 'Waving through a broken window at the bottom of the carriage, and cries were heard. More than one voice. We used megaphones from the bridge and the ground to order anyone else in the carriage to stay as still as possible while we tried to stablise things.' He cleared his throat. 'Nothing's been seen or heard since.'

'Needs triaging, then,' Mac said calmly. 'How stable is the bridge?'

'Engineers reckon it's safe at each end, which is where the cables have been anchored. For some reason there was a structural collapse towards the middle, which is what's caused the incident. According to an eye witness who was driving on the road over there, carriage 3 was swinging violently when the first carriages broke free. Presumably it's fairly well caught up to have stayed there but it's anyone's guess how long the connection's going to last.'

'Incident' was such an insignificant title for this disaster. Julia sucked in a breath as she looked up again. The carriage had gone careening off the rails. There must have been one hell of a jolt and then it would have been swinging wildly. Passengers would have been hurled about like puppets and the potential for serious, if not fatal injuries was high.

Her gaze narrowed. The carriage had windows

and a door at either end. The door at the top was still open, leaving a black hole that would be an easy entrance. She shifted her gaze back to the men beside her.

'We can winch down from the bridge and have a look.'

There was a heartbeat's silence after Julia had spoken. They all knew it was unlikely they would see as much as they needed to through the windows and impossible to assess the condition let alone treat victims, but if someone climbed inside it would mean disengaging from any safety of a winch line.

This was dangerous. Very dangerous. Weird that Julia's nerves seemed to have vanished.

'I can do that,' she said.

Both men stared at her. Mac opened his mouth to say something but Julia was faster.

'I'm half your weight,' she said. 'We don't know how much movement those cables are going to cope with and it would be sensible to use whatever advantages we've got. The more gently we can test it, the safer we're all going to be.'

'We've got a crane on the way,' the scene commander added. 'The plan was to lower the carriage to ground level.'

'How long will that take to get here?'

The man responsible for overseeing this enormous scene sighed. 'At least three hours. Maybe longer.'

Too long for anyone struggling to survive in there. Way too long.

Mac's eyes narrowed as he assessed the scene again. Then his gaze was on her and it was just as penetrating. Julia held the touch of those dark eyes with her own and waited. Patiently. She had learned that nothing else she said would make any difference now.

This was Mac's call as the senior officer and she trusted his judgment.

The eye contact went on…and on. Long enough for it to have been unacceptable between people who didn't know each other extremely well indeed. Long enough for it to be intimate but not uncomfortable because they both knew what this was about and it was purely professional.

OK, it was deeply personal as well, of course, because they relied on each other and this was about life-and-death decisions being made— for themselves and others—but they both knew where the boundaries lay and they'd never stepped close enough to even have to define those limits.

Questions were being asked and answered here.

'Are you sure about this?'

'Yes.'

'You don't have to.'

'I know.'

'This will be the toughest yet.'

'I know that too. I can do this, Mac.'

'I know you can.'

And, finally, there it was. Mac's nod.

Slow but resolute. Permission had been granted.

She hadn't expected him to agree so easily.

The flicker of surprise had been there in her

eyes. Mac had registered gratitude, too, for the respect his decision encompassed. What he hadn't seen, and which would have been entirely understandable, had been a hint of dismay that he wasn't going to use his authority to stop her tackling this incredibly dangerous mission.

Julia Bennett was one astonishing woman.

Did they breed them all like this in that little country at the bottom of the world? Pint-sized Amazons with rapier-sharp brains and a courage too deep to measure?

No. Mac checked the buckles on Julia's harness and tugged at the carabiner on the front one last time before moving to where he intended to operate the winch. This woman was a one-off. Totally unique. The first female to get through the rigorous selection process to gain access to this elite rescue squad, and he'd been lucky enough to be designated her partner.

Not that he'd felt like that first up, mind you. Neither had any of the guys on the other shifts. Mac had seen the relief in the glances exchanged at that team briefing so many weeks ago now.

A foreigner was fine. They had people from all corners of the globe on staff. But a *girl*?

Not that a twenty-eight-year-old could be considered anything less than a woman but her lack of height made her seem much younger. It didn't help that she had such a pretty, fragile kind of prettiness about her either. The spikes of that practical, pixie haircut did nothing to disguise her femininity and if the big, blue eyes that went with those blonde spikes could look like they did with no make-up, it was obvious that Jules could be a knock-out if she chose to be.

Nobody had expected to find that she considered herself 'one of the boys' and was possibly more passionate about this job than they were. She had earned respect remarkably quickly, thanks to an early job that had involved a large portion of the squad when the remains of an old building had collapsed on a demolition crew. Julia had been the only one small enough to squeeze through a gap and she'd hung, upside down, like a determined little bat, for long enough to establish an airway and gain IV access on a man who would certainly have died otherwise.

Respect had become admiration from more than one of the guys but the polite rebuff of any personal overtures had added another dimension to a personality that was intriguing. Any commiseration Mac had received on being partnered with 'the chick' had long since morphed into envy.

Yeah…he was lucky.

But here he was, letting this amazing woman step backwards off a broken bridge, his fingers on the controls that were now lowering her close to the dangling train carriage. If it fell, it would most likely take her with it and there would be nothing he could do but watch. The tension was growing by the second as the small figure in the orange overalls slipped lower.

'Keep going.' Julia's voice sounded clear and calm inside his helmet. 'Seats are clear at the top. I can't see the bottom yet.'

He fed out the steel cable, inch by inch. He felt the jerk as Julia's steel-capped boots touched the side of the carriage and then her gloved hands reached to steady herself and cut the light reflecting on one of the large glass panels.

'Stop!' The command was sharp. 'I can see something.'

CHAPTER TWO

FACES.

Terrified faces. A huddle of humanity in what had been one end of the carriage and was now a narrow base. It was too dark to see clearly. Now mid-afternoon on a typical, drizzly autumn day, natural light was fading fast but the light on Julia's helmet could only go so far through the barrier of glass and deep shadow within. The first two rows of the seats now facing upwards had people on them and were much easier to see. The closest figure was lying slumped.

More people were huddled on the seats on the other side of the aisle.

How many were there?

How badly injured were they?

Julia could see them watching her. A woman on the far side, with a child clutched in her arms, was sobbing but the sound wasn't reaching through the window that was still intact on this side. Or not through the padding inside her helmet and the background noise that included a helicopter hovering directly overhead.

Television crews, probably, capturing the unfolding drama of this rescue. The footage would make international news, that was for sure. Julia spared a fleeting thought for the relatives of everyone involved. Including hers. Thank goodness her sister Anne would be unable to recognise that it was her doing such a dangerous job.

'Can you hear me?' Julia shouted.

'Ouch!' came Mac's voice.

'Sorry.' Julie lifted her microphone, tucking it under the rim of her helmet. She called again and a boy inside, who looked about fourteen, nodded warily.

'How many of you are there?' Julia called.

The boy's eyes slid sideways but he didn't move his head. He looked hunched. Terrified of moving, probably, in case it was enough to send the carriage plummeting to the bottom of the gully. He shrugged helplessly and then winced and Julia could see the way he was cradling one arm with the other. A fracture? Dislocated shoulder?

The woman who had been sobbing in the seat across the aisle tried to get closer, the child still in her arms. She was blocked by the still shape of the slumped man.

'*Help*!' she screamed. 'Please...*help* us!'

Her words were clearly audible. So was the panicked response from others still in there, telling her to stay still, prompted by the sway of the carriage her movement had caused. Julia's hands were still against the window and she simply moved with it, gently swinging out and then back. Not far at all but more than enough for her heart to skip a beat and for a soft curse from Mac to echo in her earphones.

Julia flipped down the small arm of her microphone. 'Pull me up to the door, Mac. I need to get inside.'

'No way!'

'Can't triage from here. I can see at least six people and some look OK to evacuate fast.'

'Get them to climb up and we'll winch from the door.'

Julia frowned. The woman was close to hysterical and wasn't about to let go of the child. The teenage boy had an injured arm or shoulder.

'Not practical,' she informed Mac. 'They need assistance. Anyone else qualified to operate the winch up there?'

'Yes.' The word was reluctant. 'Red Watch is here now as well.'

Another SERT partnership of Angus and Dale. This was good.

'I'll get inside,' Julia suggested. 'You winch down with a nappy harness and I'll bring out as many as I can. Then we'll be able to assess what we've got left.'

Mac must have shifted his microphone but Julia could hear faint voices in animated conversation and knew that her idea was being discussed with others up there on the bridge. A long minute later and Mac was ready to talk to her again.

'On one condition,' he said briskly. 'We're monitoring the cables. We might not get much warning if things aren't going to hold but if I give the word you have to get yourself out of there. Stat. No argument. Got it?'

'Got it.'

Julia did get it and her promise of co-operation was sincere. She heard the faint wail of distress as she was hoisted away from the faces at the bottom of the carriage despite her hand signals to indicate that things were in hand and rescue was close.

And then there she was. Beside the door. She had to climb inside and unclip the winch line that suddenly felt like an umbilical cord in its ability to sustain life.

Fear kicked in as she did precisely that. Her mouth went dry and her heart pounded so hard it was almost painful. For a horribly long moment, Julia thought she'd gone too far this time. She couldn't do this after all.

'Jules? Talk to me.'

The voice was soft but she could hear a faint reflection of her own fear. Mac was afraid for *her* and it was more than concern for the well-being of his colleague. Or was that just wishful thinking on her part?

Stupidly—and so inappropriately it was easy to contain—Julia felt an odd tightness in her throat. A prickle behind her eyes that advertised embryonic tears. She dismissed them with a simple swallow. She didn't need to go there. All she'd needed had been to hear his voice. To remind herself that she wasn't doing this alone. That she had the best possible person in the world watching her back right now.

'I'm…inside,' she relayed. 'Climbing down.' She moved as she spoke. Cautiously. Hanging onto the back of a seat frame as her feet found purchase on the cushioned back of the next seat down the vertical aisle. 'How are those cables looking, mate?'

'Good,' came the terse response. Mac was concentrating as hard as she was.

'These seats make quite a good ladder.' Julia kept talking because she wanted Mac to keep responding. She wanted to hear his voice. Maybe she needed to keep hearing it because it gave her more courage than she could ever otherwise summon.

But when she was halfway down the aisle, the smell hit her. The smell of fear. And she could hear the voices and moans and she knew that within seconds she would be able to speak to and touch these unfortunate people. She could start doing the job she was trained to do and help those who had been plunged into a nightmare they couldn't deal with alone.

Julia felt the power that came with the knowledge that *she* could help and that power gave her complete focus. Knowing that Mac was close gave her strength, yes, but that was simply a platform now. This was it.

Time to go to work.

'Who can hear me?' she called, pausing briefly. 'Keep still but raise your hand if you can.'

She wanted to count. To find out how many were conscious enough to hear her and physically capable of any movement at all.

One hand went up tentatively. And then there was another. And another. Six? No, seven. And dim patches where she could see the shape of people but no hands. The less injured people would have to be evacuated first to allow access to the others.

The woman she'd earlier deemed close to hysteria was still sobbing. 'Please…' she called back. 'Take Carla first. She's only seven… *Please*!'

Julia revised her count to eight. Carla was being clutched too tightly to have raised her hand.

She climbed closer. The teenage boy with the injured arm was silent but she was close enough to see that his eyes were locked on her progress. Searching for her face. Silently pleading with as much passion as Carla's mother.

Julia had to tear her gaze away to try and reassess the number and condition of victims she would be dealing with. To triage the whole scene, but it was difficult. The light had faded even more outside now and it was much darker in here. The light on her helmet could only illuminate a patch at a time and it was like trying to put a mental jigsaw together.

People were jumbled together. Right now it was impossible to see which limbs belonged to which person or even how many people were in the tangle.

'Get me out!' A male voice from behind Carla and her mother was loud. 'I can't feel my legs. I need help.'

Julia saw hands come over the seat back behind the still sobbing woman. Good grief, was the man trying to move himself despite possible spinal or neck injuries? Someone beside him groaned and then someone else screamed as the man's frantic efforts created a shuffle of movement and made the carriage swing alarmingly.

'Stay absolutely *still*, and I mean everybody!' Julia injected every ounce of authority she could into the command. 'Listen to me,' she continued, her tone softening a little. 'I know you're all scared but you've all been incredibly brave for a long time and I need you all to hang onto that courage so you can help me do my job.'

Carla's mother sniffed and fixed wide eyes on Julia. She would do anything, her gaze said. Anything that would, at least, save her child. The man behind her was quiet. Hopefully listening. Even a groan from nearby sounded as if someone was doing their best to stifle the involuntary interruption.

'We're going to get you all out,' Julia said confidently, 'but we have to do this carefully. One at a time. I'm going to help anyone who can move to get to the top of the carriage where someone will be waiting to carry them up to the bridge.'

Would Mac be there yet? Dangling on a winch line with a harness in his hands that he would pass through the door to Julia to buckle onto each survivor?

'I'm here, Jules.' It wasn't the first time that

Mac had seemed to be able to read her thoughts. 'Ready when you are.'

'When we've got as many as we can out, we'll be able to take care of all of you that are injured and we'll get you out as well,' Julia told the passengers. 'Do you all understand? Can you help me?'

She heard a whimper of fear and another groan but amongst the sounds of suffering came assent.

'Just get on with it!' the loud man was pleading now. 'Stop talking and *do* something.'

Julia climbed past another seat. She made sure her feet were secure and then anchored herself with one hand. 'Pass Carla to me,' she ordered.

'*No-o-o-o*!' the child shrieked.

'You *have* to, baby.' With tears streaming down her face but her voice remarkably calm, Carla's mother peeled small arms from around her neck and pushed her child towards Julia. 'I'll be there soon, I promise.' Her voice broke on the last word but Julia now had a small girl clinging her like a terrified monkey and she didn't take the time to reassure the mother. She was climbing upwards again and part of her brain was planning ahead. The teenage boy next. She had a triangular bandage in the neat pack belted to her hips. She could secure his injured arm and he should be able to climb with her. Maybe Carla's mother after that, so that her panic wouldn't make it harder for everyone else to wait their turn.

There would be others after that and then the real work could begin. Assessing and stabilising the injured and getting them out of here and on the way to definitive medical care.

By then the weight in the carriage and the potential for unexpected movement would be well down. The cables would have had a reasonably thorough test. Mac or one of the other SERT guys could join her. Someone would have to because there was no way she could carry the injured up herself.

Carrying a slight, seven-year-old girl was proving hard enough. The extra weight made it an effort to balance and then push up to the next padded rung of this odd ladder of seats. Julia's breathing was becoming labored and the muscles in her legs and arms were burning. She had to concentrate more with every step so that fatigue wouldn't cause a slip that might send them both falling down the central aisle.

She couldn't even afford the extra effort of looking up past her burden to see how close she was to the top or whether Mac was peering down to watch her progress.

'You're almost there. Two more.'

How did he *do* that? Know precisely when she needed encouragement? This time, he could probably see the way she hesitated before each upward push. How each hesitation was becoming a little longer so he wasn't really mind-reading. It just felt like that.

She could do two more. No. Julia could feel the determined line of her lips twist into a kind of smile. She could do *ten* more knowing that Mac was waiting at the top.

'Good job.'

The quiet words were praise enough for her efforts. Julia was too breathless to respond immediately, though. She simply nodded once and then held out her hand for the nappy harness. Then she edged—carefully—into the first space of upturned seats so that she could sit and use both arms and hands for her next task.

'It's OK, sweetheart,' she told the rigid bundle on her lap. 'I'm going to put these special straps around you and then Mac's going to get you out of here and carry you right up to the top.'

'No-o-o!' Arms tightened their vice-like grip around Julia's neck.

'I need to go back and look after the other people. Like your mummy. You'll be fine, Carla, I promise.'

But the child was shaking now. Whimpering with fear.

'Mac is a *very* nice man,' Julia told her.

'Cheers, mate,' came with the chuckle in her earphones.

'And he really, really likes children,' Julia

added. 'Looking after little girls like you is absolutely his favourite thing to do.'

The earphones stayed silent this time. What was Mac thinking? Remembering occasions when he'd poured his heart and soul into trying to save a child? The heartbreak when he hadn't been successful?

Carla had relaxed fractionally. Enough for Julia to be able to slip the straps into position and then close and tighten buckles. She hoped the silence wasn't because Mac was putting two and two together somehow. That he had noticed at some point over the last weeks the way she avoided prolonged contact with paediatric patients if possible. The way she was so good at distancing herself by taking on any case that was preferably complicated *and* adult.

No. She was pretty confident she kept personal issues well away from her work. Out of her life, in fact, because she wasn't letting anyone close enough to discover the truth.

'I'm going to tell Mummy how brave you are,'

Julia told Carla. 'As soon as I get back down to her. Do you think she'll be proud of you?'

Carla didn't nod but her head moved so that she could look up at Julia.

'*I'm* proud of you.' Julia smiled. 'Mac will be, too, you'll see.'

She eased herself to her feet. Carla was still tense and she cried out in terror when Julia lifted her into Mac's waiting hands but then she was in his strong, secure grasp and the child looked up and saw the face of the man above her.

Mac's smile was as reassuring as a hug.

'Hi, there, peanut,' he said. 'Going to come for a wee ride with me?'

And this time Carla nodded and, as Mac clipped the buckle of her harness to his own and instructed the child to put her arms around his neck and hold on tight, she turned her head and Julia could see that she was—incredibly— smiling herself.

Mac was simply the best when it came to dealing with children. It had made it easier to step back herself and not get people asking awkward questions.

'Your job,' she could say to Mac with total sincerity. *'You're the best.'*

He was. He adored kids and she knew him, while he probably wouldn't admit it on station, he was aching for some of his own. And why not? He was in his mid-thirties and by now the absolute obsession with his career had to be ebbing enough for him to realise he might be running out of time to find someone to make a family with. He needed to get on with it.

He'd have gorgeous children and he'd make the best father ever.

And some incredibly lucky woman was going to be his wife and the mother of those children.

Julia turned and began climbing back down as soon as she saw Mac and Carla beginning their upward journey. She had to be just as slow and careful as she had been the first time she had done this despite it seeming easier having done it before. She couldn't afford to fall.

The descent was too slow. It allowed too much time for errant thoughts and emotions to seep into her mind and body.

Inappropriate things but she was learning to expect the backwash that came from seeing Mac with a child in his arms.

A mix of grief. And jealousy. And...yes... desire.

And, as usual, they had to be stamped out with fierce determination because there was nothing Julia could do to change the way things were now.

Not a single thing.

It took well over an hour for her to help the eight relatively uninjured victims up to the door where they had been winched up to the bridge and into the care of waiting rescuers. Eight heavy people who had required assistance to make the climb. Constant guidance and encouragement, if not actual physical support. Julia had to be exhausted both physically and mentally.

'Angus and Dale could take over the next stage,' Mac suggested.

'No way.' Julia was heading for the base of the carriage again and the crisp words via the communication system put paid to any further suggestions on Mac's part. 'The job's nearly done and there's no way I'm deserting Ken. He knows me, now.'

And she knew. She was deeply involved in this scenario and, knowing Jules, she would be committed to the people and the mission a thousand per cent. If they wanted to get her out of there it would be neither easy nor pleasant. And she was right, the job was nearly done. She had managed to get virtually all the people from the carriage out and Mac knew there was one conscious, injured person, one unconscious and one dead.

So Mac went in to join her because Julia was his partner and everybody knew just how tight a team these two were these days. Inseparable. And darned good at their jobs.

This time when Mac came down on the winch

line he brought equipment and the medical supplies they would need.

The bottom two rows of upturned seats had become a kind of triage station.

Julia indicated one of her patients. 'This man has been unconscious since I got my first glance inside.'

The figure was slumped on the seat by the window but Mac could see the end of a plastic OP airway in his mouth. Julia had obviously assessed him and done what she could in the brief window of time that triaging allowed for.

'Head injury,' Julia continued. 'GCS 3. Rapid, weak pulse and query Cheyne-Stokes breathing pattern.'

The man was very seriously injured, then. Unlikely to survive. If they took the time to evacuate him first, others who could survive might die.

'And this is Ken.' Julia was hanging onto the edge of the seat across the aisle now. 'Spinal injury. Paralysis of both legs and paresthesia in both hands.'

A high spinal injury, then. He would need very careful immobilisation before evacuation so they didn't exacerbate the injury.

Julia dropped lower, shining the light of her helmet on the very end of the carriage.

'Status zero here,' she told Mac quietly. 'There were several people on top of him to start with. He's too heavy for me to shift but I've moved enough to be fairly sure there's no one underneath him.'

Mac reached down and caught the arm and shoulder of the heavy body, lifting it further than Julia would have managed. A jumble of luggage, personal possessions like books and drink bottles filled a fair bit of space but there was no sign of movement that might indicate a survivor struggling to get out. He could see shards of broken glass in the debris as well. And so much blood he felt a familiar knot tighten in his gut. He let the man's body fall back gently.

'Let's deal with what we've got first.'

Julia nodded. 'Ken first?'

Mac agreed. The sooner they had his spine

immobilised and protected, the better the outcome might be for him.

Julia wriggled into a position where she could support Ken's head while Mac went to get the equipment they would need. A neck collar and survival blankets to start with. Oxygen and IV gear and pain relief. He found her squashed into the tiny gap beside Ken, ready to take the collar and ease it into position, and it wasn't the first time he thought it was a blessing that she was so little and mobile. There was no way he could have managed that feat so competently.

'Do you think I've broken my *neck*?' Ken sounded terrified.

'This is a precaution,' Julia reassured him. 'We don't know what part of your spine has been injured and we need to keep it all in line. It's really important that you don't move even after the collar's secured because the rest of your back isn't protected yet. We'll do everything we can but we need you to help too. Can you do that?'

The huff of sound was still fearful. 'I guess.'

'Just hang in there, mate. You're doing really, really well.'

Mac was busy opening packages but he could hear the smile in Julia's voice as she reassured her patient. He knew exactly how her face would be looking as she spoke even though he couldn't see it. Ken probably couldn't see it either. He might see the way her lips curved back into her cheeks but he wouldn't be able to see the way Julia's eyes always smiled right along with her mouth. The way her whole face—even her whole body sometimes—seemed connected to her emotional state.

Fascinating to watch. Or provoke. Mac wasn't the only one on station who took pleasure in engaging Julia in an animated discussion.

Or delight in making her smile.

'We're going to give you something for that pain very soon.' Julia was swabbing a patch on Ken's forearm. 'Wee scratch coming up. There. All done. Wasn't so bad, was it?'

'Didn't feel a thing. You know what you're doing, don't you, lassie?'

Julia chuckled. 'Sure do. Now, are you allergic to any drugs that you know of?'

Mac flicked the top of an ampoule to move the fluid inside. Then he snapped it and slid a needle into the narrow neck to draw up the drug.

Ken was right. Julia knew what she was doing. He was right, too. She was involved in this scenario to the extent that it would have been detrimental to try and give her a break. She had established a connection with Ken and he was in exactly the right frame of mind to co-operate with whatever measures needed to be taken to rescue him.

He trusted Julia and Mac knew the trust wasn't misplaced. He had to feel completely dependent on her right now but he knew that she would be treating his vulnerability with the same kind of compassion and skill she brought to the medical practices he had witnessed her administering.

She fitted an oxygen mask onto Ken and hooked it up to the small cylinder from the pack. 'I won't run fluids,' she told Mac. 'BP's down but it's more likely to be neurogenic than hypo-volaemic shock.'

'What does that mean?' Ken asked fear-fully.

'Any injury to the spine can interfere with nerves,' Julia told him. 'That's why you can't feel your legs at the moment and you're get-ting pins and needles in your hands. It's not necessarily permanent,' she added firmly, as though she'd given this reassurance more than once. 'We can't know what damage there is but what we can do is take care not to make it any worse.'

A lot of care had to go into the next stage of this rescue. They had to get Ken flat and secured onto a stretcher without twisting or bending his vertebrae. Then they would have to cushion his head and strap him so securely onto a stretcher there would be no danger of movement during the extrication process.

Minutes ticked past swiftly. Mac could feel ex-haustion biding its time, waiting for an opportu-nity to ambush him, and he knew that Julia had to be a long way further down that track. Not that she was slowing down, of course. She never did. Mac was proud of his partner. Not just for her endurance or the way she had crawled into the cramped space by the window to hold Ken's head to support his neck but for the way she effortlessly turned her skills to emotional support for their patient.

'Glasgow's home for you, isn't it, Ken?' she asked.

'Aye. I was just going up to Inverness on business for the day.'

'What do you do?'

'My company makes umbrellas.'

Julia chuckled. 'You must be doing really well. I've never seen so much rain as I have in the three months I've been here.'

'Where are you from?'

'New Zealand.'

'That's a country I've always wanted to visit. Is it as beautiful as they say it is?'

Mac found himself nodding. He felt exactly the same way. He'd love to get down to the bottom of the world for a visit. Always had, but the urge had got a lot stronger in the last few months. Funny, that.

'It is,' Julia was saying. 'Parts of it are very similar to Scotland but I think we get a bit more sunshine.'

'You going back?'

'Yes. I work with an ambulance service that has a rescue unit back home. I'm here for six months for advanced training.'

'What part of New Zealand do you live in?'

'Christchurch. Middle of the south island. We've got the Alps to the west and the sea to the east. I grew up there.'

'You've got family to go home to, then.' Ken's voice wobbled. He was obviously thinking of his own family and feeling alone right now.

'Only my big sister,' Julia told him.

Mac was busy pulling the extrication device they needed from its case but he was listening carefully. This was personal information. The kind that Jules had kept from her colleagues. He might have been left with questions that would never be answered but Ken wanted distraction from his situation. And Julia was so involved, she probably hadn't registered that others might be able to hear.

'She's like a mum, really,' she told Ken. 'My mother died shortly after I was born. Anne's nearly seven years older than me and she just took over from the various nannies. When Dad died I was only eleven but Anne was old enough to take care of me. She's amazing. Managed to raise me and get through med school at the same time. I love her to bits.'

There was a short silence then. Julia appeared to be checking Ken's pulse. Or was she holding his hand?

'When you get to New Zealand,' she said then, 'make sure you visit Christchurch. It's a very English city but don't hold that against it, will you?'

Something suspiciously like a sniffle could be heard from Ken. 'Nay, lassie,' he said. 'I won't.'

He hadn't missed the conviction in Julia's tone

that he would, someday, be well enough to travel to the other side of the world. She had deepened the connection between them by sharing personal information and now her confidence was a boost. She was his anchor right now. Nothing more personal was said because she shifted to professional responsibilities, making sure Ken was fully informed and understood everything going on around him to keep his fear at bay.

'We're getting something called a KED around you now, Ken. You'll feel us tipping you a bit so we can slide it underneath.'

'But I'm not supposed to move!'

'I've got you. Relax. I won't let anything happen to your alignment.'

'What did you say it was?'

'It's like a body splint. It goes right round your chest and waist and up behind your neck and then we do up a whole bunch of straps. Then it'll be safe to get you on the stretcher and out of here.'

'It's dark now, isn't it?'

'Pretty much. Don't worry. We'll have lights

all over the place out there now. We can see what we're doing.'

Sure enough, massive lights had been put in place both on the ground and the bridge and, despite drizzle that was determined to become rain, the visibility was excellent. It was still a slow job extricating Ken. He had pain relief on board and was completely immobilised but even the tiniest movement hurt. Angus joined them inside the carriage but it still took an age to inch the stretcher carefully upwards. Julia stayed as close as she could to Ken's head. Talking to him. Reassuring him. Sympathising with the amount of pain he was in. It needed extra help to get the stretcher out of the door and attached to the winch and while that was happening Mac checked the harness he still wore in preparation to accompany the stretcher.

But Julia had other ideas.

'I'll go up with him.'

What he could see of her face looked very pale. Pinched, almost, as though she had been doing more than reassuring Ken and had actually taken some of his pain on board. Mac shook the thought off but whatever the cause she was reaching the limits of her endurance and steadying a stretcher being winched to make sure it didn't catch on obstacles, not to mention helping to lift it over the lip of the destination, was no mean feat.

'I think *I* should,' was all he said.

But then he looked down from Julia's face to where her hand was holding Ken's. To the way Ken was looking up at Julia, his fear only just contained. And, for a weird moment, Mac felt envious. Of that connection. Of that touch.

'OK,' he amended a little hurriedly. 'If you're sure.'

Julia gave a single nod. 'I'm sure.'

There were hand-held television cameras on the bridge now. Journalists eager to interview Julia as Ken was transferred to waiting paramedic crews who had a helicopter ready to evacuate him.

'You're going to the best spinal unit in Glasgow

for assessment,' Julia was able to tell Ken as she said goodbye. 'I'll come and visit you very soon.'

She avoided the media, pushing back to watch anxiously as her SERT colleagues brought out the man with the serious head injury, who was, amazingly, still clinging to life, and were then winched up themselves, one by one. By the time Mac joined her on the bridge, they had been on scene for nearly five hours and their official shift had finished some time ago.

Not that any of them were about to leave just yet. The weather was closing in and the transport that had taken Ken to Glasgow had been the last that would be leaving by air. Joe was grounded so they would have to organise road transport to get back to station and the people who could do that for them were otherwise occupied because the crane had finally arrived and the last stages of this rescue were under way.

Things hadn't quite ended. It made no difference that they had started this shift well over twelve hours ago and that they were both exhausted. This had become 'their' job and they would see it through to the bitter end.

Had she known how bitter that end would be, Julia thought later, she would never have been so willing to accompany Mac back to the carriage for a final check. She would have found some way to ensure that someone other than them were the last people present.

The dead body was sprawled flat on the floor now, debris strewn under, around and over him. Julia edged in beside a seat to give the men in orange overalls room to load the man onto a stretcher and carry him to the temporary morgue set up in one of the huge tents. A space she knew already had fourteen occupants from this disaster.

She watched in silence as the stretcher was eased through the door and outside into the bleak night. Then she turned her head to see Mac also watching. Unguarded for an instant as the beam of her headlamp caught his face, she could see his exhaustion and the kind of defeat that went with every life lost on their watch.

Then he stooped and picked something up from the debris that had been pushed into piles to make way for the stretcher. Julia focused on what he held. It was a soft toy animal of some kind. Probably well loved and shabby to start with but it now had stuffing coming from a ripped-off leg and it was covered with blood-stains.

'Carla's, do you think?'

'Probably. We didn't have any other children in the carriage, thank goodness.'

For a long moment, she held Mac's gaze. Watching the wheels turning in a brain shrugging off how tired it was. For a moment she wondered if he was thinking her statement was another indication of her aversion to working with paediatric cases but then she saw the grim lines in his face deepen and a haunted look appear in the way he frowned. There was another possibility.

They both turned to look back at the space the dead man had filled.

At the door that had been blocked by the body.

It was Mac who moved to open it. He had to put his shoulder against it and push because it was blocked from the inside. And then Julia heard him curse, softly but vehemently, as he dropped instantly to a crouch.

Her view was limited to what she could see over his shoulder because Mac filled the narrow doorway. She could see narrow shoulders and the back of a head covered with long, blonde hair. A woman, then. Had she been thrown to hit her head against the basin during the violent change of direction as the carriage had tipped? Except that there was no obvious injury to be seen from this angle.

Mac had his hand on her neck, searching for a pulse.

'She's too cold.' Mac's voice sounded raw. 'Been dead for a fair while.'

At least there hadn't been a child in here as well. Julia still had to swallow hard as she reached for the portable radio clipped to her belt. 'I'll let the guys know to bring the stretcher back.'

'Wait!' Mac was examining the woman, looking for an indication of what might have killed her. He found nothing.

'Pelvis?' Julia suggested.

Mac put his hands on the woman's hips and pressed. Julia knew it would have been a gentle test but she could see the movement. There were major blood vessels running through that area. If one was cut it was quite possible to bleed to death in a short space of time.

It was also possible they might have been able to save her if they'd got to her first.

Mac was pressing a hand to the woman's abdomen now. It was distended. Even more distended than they might have expected from all the internal bleeding.

'Oh, *God*!' Mac groaned.

Julia didn't ask. She didn't need to. The shape was too regular and obviously too firm to be simply an accumulation of blood. The woman had probably only been in the early stages of her pregnancy but there had been two lives lost here.

Mac straightened. He didn't meet Julia's horrified gaze.

'It's time we went home,' he said heavily. 'There's nothing more we can do here.'

CHAPTER THREE

SOMETHING wasn't right.

They should have been able to debrief and put things into perspective on the long road trip back to headquarters courtesy of a military vehicle. They could have talked through how impossible it would have been to save that young woman. Even if they'd known she was there, they would still have had to evacuate all the mobile people and the time needed to shift the dead man and then extricate her would have put Ken in more trouble. And they couldn't have known. There wasn't even a window that Julia could have looked into from the outside.

These were things that should have been said aloud. Dissected and come to terms with. And maybe then they could have congratulated themselves on a job well done. The fact that ten people had made it out alive when it could have gone in a very different direction and claimed even more victims.

But Mac, for the first time Julia had known him, didn't want to talk and that was confusing. He was the strongest, bravest man she had ever met. Six feet tall in his socks and without an ounce of fat on his body. His strength alone was enough to inspire confidence Julia couldn't hope to impart as soon as he arrived on scene. But there was more to Mac than physical attributes. He was so open and honest and always smiling. Smiling so much that he had deep crinkles around his eyes and grooves on his cheeks. She had seen him tired beyond exhaustion. Frustrated enough to be angry. Sad, even, to the point of his voice sounding thick with tears, but she'd never seen him quite like this.

'I'm stuffed,' he said, when she tried to get him to talk at the start of their road trip home. 'I need sleep. Let's leave the talking till later, OK?'

Which would have been fine, except that Mac didn't sleep. Neither could Julia, Not after she'd noticed the way he was staring through the window on his side. Lost in thoughts he obviously didn't want to share and looking so...bleak.

He closed his eyes, later, but he was feigning sleep. Julia could tell because she could see the way his hands were clenched into fists. So tense.

She wanted—badly—to touch him. To find out what was bothering him and—somehow—make it better.

She cared, dammit. Too much.

And so she said nothing. She kept to her side of the back seat and stared out of *her* window. Her body ached with weariness and more than a few bumps and bruises but her heart ached more.

For Mac.

Ten years.

It had been a decade ago and Mac hadn't even thought about it for eons.

What was it about that moment that had brought it back so vividly?

The long blonde hair?

The early pregnancy?

Or was it because Julia had been standing so close to him?

It was like pieces of a jigsaw he hadn't intended, or wanted, to solve had come together out of nowhere.

Mac could hear the suck of heavy-duty tyres on water-soaked roadways along with the rumble of the engine and the background buzz of the radio station the driver was listening to. Runnels of water coalesced on the window and then streaked sideways but Mac wasn't really watching. He was seeing an altogether different picture.

No wonder he found Julia Bennett so damned attractive on so many levels. It wasn't just that she was gorgeous and smart and brave. It was that full-on approach to life in combination with an ability to sidestep any hint of a meaningful personal relationship that did it.

Presented the kind of challenge any red-blooded man would find irresistible, it was almost a matter of honour to have a crack at winning such a prize. Or wanting to.

Why hadn't he put two and two together before this?

Because he'd done his damnedest to forget Christine, that was why. To forget the heartache of absolute failure. To move on and make a success of his life.

'You OK, mate?' Julia had asked when they were on the main road and settling in for their journey back to headquarters.

'I'm stuffed,' he'd growled. And he was. Exhausted both physically and emotionally. In pain, actually, because something raw had been unexpectedly exposed deep within. He'd never talked to anyone about it. Ever. And if he did, Julia would be at the bottom of any list of potential listeners. He wasn't about to admit the kind of failure he was on a personal level. Preferably not to anyone but especially not to a woman whom he doubted had ever failed at anything and who would be less than impressed with a man who was nowhere near her equal.

'I need sleep,' he'd added tonelessly, turning away from her. 'Let's leave the talking till later, OK?'

She accepted his withdrawal and why wouldn't she? Today had been tough. This was the best job in the world but it took a day when they succeeded a hundred per cent to reinforce that. A job when no one died or got maimed for life. The way through feeling like that was to talk about it, of course. He knew that. Debriefing was ingrained in anyone who worked in careers that dealt with this kind of trauma and degree of human suffering. It was a part of the job, really, to analyse everything that had happened. To take a quiet pride in things that had been done well and to learn from anything else so they could go out and do an even better job next time.

But he couldn't talk to Julia about this. Not yet. Not when he'd been blindsided by memories and could see danger signs a mile high. Signs that warned him how easy it would be to fall in love with this woman. Hell, he was already quite a way down that track and hadn't even noticed.

He couldn't afford to let her anywhere near him right now, when the scab over that failure had been ripped off and he was feeling raw. Vulnerable, even, and Alan MacCulloch didn't do vulnerable, thanks very much. Imagine if she wasn't unimpressed with his history. If she accepted him, warts and all. He'd fall. Hard. In a way he'd managed to avoid for a whole decade. Nearly a quarter of his life, come to think of it.

She didn't want that.

Neither did he.

Julia was looking at him. He could feel it. He could sense her concern, like a gust of warmth crossing the gap on the back seat in the back of this vehicle. She wanted to offer comfort but Mac didn't want that either. He closed his eyes and pretended to sleep.

Well after midnight, they got back to the outskirts of Glasgow and the station they shared with a road-based ambulance service. They collected their packs from the back of the truck.

'Cheers, mate,' Julia said to the soldier who'd been their chauffeur. 'Hope you get to go back to base and get some shuteye now.'

'Not a chance.' The young soldier grinned. 'I've got to get back to the scene. We'll be there until it's all cleaned up.'

Cleaning up was exactly what he and Julia needed to do. Mac picked up his pack and swung it onto his back. From the corner of his eye he could see Julia struggling to do the same. She was so tired she could barely stay upright, poor thing. The urge to look after her was far too strong to ignore.

'Here,' he said gruffly. 'I'll take them. You go and hit the showers.'

'No, thanks.' The tone was cool. 'I can manage.'

She gave up on lifting the pack to her back and just held it in her arms instead, turning away without a glance in his direction.

It was a slap he deserved so he had no right to feel hurt. Julia had done nothing wrong and hadn't deserved to be treated the way he had treated her. God, how selfish had he been? Maybe she'd been the one who needed the debrief. Praise, if nothing else, for her extraordinary courage and endurance.

He'd made a mistake. A big one. How hard would it have been to talk about the job like they always did? Made a few jokes, even. The kind of black humour that diffused the dark space they were all in danger of slipping into with this kind of job. He could have made her smile and that would have made *him* smile and feel good. She would never have guessed that he'd been thinking of anything other than work.

He'd been stupid as well as selfish. Not only had he created an uncomfortable distance between himself and his partner, it had been the worst defence possible for himself. He'd had nothing to do but think for nearly two hours. Sitting there being so aware of the woman sitting beside him. Wanting her and pushing her away simultaneously.

God, he'd never felt this tired. Exhaustion was becoming confusion. A long, hot shower was what he needed and then he'd head home. Maybe it was better not to say anything more to Jules tonight in an attempt to put things right because, the way he was feeling, he would most likely make things worse. They were due for two days off now. By the time they had to see each other again, she might have forgotten his moodiness or at least forgiven his silence. They could just go back and pick up where they'd left off.

Being colleagues who respected and cared about each other. Julia had called the soldier 'mate' and it was what she often called him as well. That's what they were. Mates. Comrades. Not quite friends because that implied something a lot more personal than they had. Dangerous territory.

The decision to leave things was a relief. The shower and change into warm, dry civvies was a comfort. Mac signed himself out and noted Julia's signature already in the logbook. She'd left before him and that was good.

Or was it?

And why was her car still in the parking lot at the back of the station?

Maybe she'd gone into the messroom to talk to the crew on night shift. Mac battled, briefly, with the desire to retrace his footsteps and find her but solved the problem by turning towards his own vehicle—a hefty, black four-wheel drive that filled his allocated space. Overflowed from it, in fact, despite him nosing it in until the front bumper virtually touched the moss of the old stone wall surrounding this area. There were trees on the other side of the wall. Big, dark shapes that created such intense shadows he didn't see Julia until he was about to pull his driver's door open.

She was sitting on the wall. Wrapped up in a padded anorak and mittens. Waiting for him.

'*What* the—?'

Julia jumped down. Her hood fell away and

she wrapped her arms around her body as she took a step forward. And then another. Until she was close enough for him to see that her hair was still damp despite the protection the hood had given her from the drizzle. Close enough for him to smell the shampoo she'd just been using.

'I couldn't go home,' she said quietly. 'Not without knowing what rattled your cage so much tonight.' Her gaze caught his and held it. 'Was it something I did?'

'Good grief, no!' Mac was transfixed. By the smell of…what was it? A mixture of soap and… almonds, that's what it was. Even more by the warmth he could feel radiating off this small, determined woman. Most of all, by the way her eyes seemed to catch the glow from the lights behind him in the parking lot. He knew her eyes were blue but right now they were just huge and dark and full of concern.

'It…it was the job,' he told her. 'It…got to me.'

'Of course it did.' A tiny nod advertised that

Julia had already come to that conclusion. 'There'd be something wrong if it didn't.' She frowned now, glancing down and lowering her voice. 'But why couldn't you talk about it? Like we always do?'

Mac opened his mouth to offer the same excuse of exhaustion. Or to say he'd been asleep but it was obvious she knew he would be lying. She was looking up at him again and he could see plainly that she knew he hadn't been asleep. She'd seen through him in the truck and she was seeing through him now. Right into his head. Into his heart. There was no escape and, suddenly, Mac didn't want to find one.

'That woman,' he heard himself saying. 'She... reminded me of someone.'

'Ahh.' The sound was long. It contained complete understanding that there was—or had been—a woman of great importance in his life. Far more important than herself.

Mac could actually see the thought process going on in the way she was standing so still she wasn't even blinking. The almost imperceptible backing away he could sense. The way her lips were parted a fraction as her mind worked.

And that slight parting of her lips was Mac's complete undoing.

She was so wrong to put herself down in any way but that was exactly what she was doing. She was convincing herself that she had been dismissed in favour of the woman he'd been thinking about. That she was somehow less worthy of his attention. So wrong, and there was only one way he could think to prove it as soon as he noticed her lips.

He had to kiss her.

She could have stopped him. Time seemed to slow down to a crawl. He looked at her mouth and then back to her eyes and he could see that she knew he was unable to resist the temptation now that the thought had occurred to him. Slowly and deliberately…so slowly she had any amount of time to duck out of reach, he tilted and lowered his head. He was giving her the chance to move. Part of him was desperately hoping she would.

But she didn't move a single muscle.

Her mouth was there. Waiting for him. Her lips still parted. And even then Mac moved so slowly he could feel the warmth of her breath against his lips before he closed that last, infinitesimal space.

Once his lips touched hers, he couldn't think of anything else at all. Her mouth claimed his. Dragged him in. Drugged him. It was only the need for oxygen that forced him to break the contact but then he heard the sound that Julia made. A soft whimper of desire and he was lost again.

When her mittened hands came up to circle his neck, he surrendered himself without a heartbeat's hesitation. He caught her head in his hands and tilted it. Touched her lips and then her tongue with his own and it felt like the ground had vanished from beneath his feet. He was weightless. Floating. Vaporised in some fashion by the heat being generated.

When he became aware of what he was

standing on again, Mac felt reality returning with a jolt. Who had broken that extraordinary kiss? He didn't think he could have if his life had depended on it.

He was breathing hard. So was Julia. She'd stepped back from him. It must have been she who had broken the contact, then, because Mac was sure his feet hadn't moved. What was she thinking? What on earth could he say that might diffuse the intensity of what had just happened? Did he want to?

And then Julia peeped up at him and grinned.

'You have to marry me now, you know,' she said.

Mac's jaw dropped but then it hit him. This was a joke. Maybe Julia's reaction to the kiss had been nothing like his own. Or maybe she was just as astonished as he was and needed enough space to get her head around it. For whatever reason, she was going to make light of it and right now, it seemed the perfect way forward.

'Hey…' He feigned shock. 'It was only a kiss.'

'Only a kiss? Cheers, Mac.'But her lips twitched and there was a glow of merriment in her eyes.

Mac's smile felt rusty but it was still there. And it grew. He could feel it stretching something that had got way too tight inside him. 'It was a pretty good kiss,' he said thoughtfully.

Julia nodded in agreement. 'Exactly.' She sighed. 'So now you have to marry me.'

Mac's smile broadened. 'Is that so?'

Julia nodded again. Firmly. 'Yep. I paid attention at school and Sister Therese *said…*'

The bark of ironic laughter came from nowhere. Oh, God…if only Julia knew that she was making a joke about the very thing that had been haunting Mac so keenly. He could actually hear a faint echo of his own voice from a decade ago.

'I'll marry you, Chris. We can make this work.'

And hers. Scathing.

'You can't be serious! You think I want a kid? Holding me back? Interfering with everything I want to do with my life?'

'It's my baby, too. You can't just—'

'It's my body, Alan. I can do whatever I like and you can't stop me.'

How could he have thought that Julia and Christine were alike? The very idea of marriage had been an insult. A threat, even, to the woman he'd believed himself in love with. Something that could never have been discussed reasonably, let alone joked about.

That Julia *could* make a joke of it was the other end of the spectrum, wasn't it? Maybe he should find that almost as offensive but, somehow, it wasn't.

She didn't know and, at this particular moment in time, it really didn't matter. How could it, in the wake of that astonishing kiss that had taken him somewhere he'd never been before? A place that held release rather than tension. A pleasure so pure it was paradise.

Relief was coursing through him as well. If

he wanted to make something out of this new development in their relationship with each other it was going to be up to him. Julia wasn't bothered. She could laugh it off. Even better, any damage done by his behaviour tonight was repaired. They would be able to work together again without a barrier that would have been unbearable.

He could play this game. He could laugh it off too and make it go away.

'Come on, then,' he said, completely deadpan. 'I've got a full tank in my car and Gretna Green isn't that far away.'

Julia laughed. She turned away, shaking her head. 'Are you kidding? I only listened to Sister Therese's rules, I didn't obey them.' She was walking away now, towards her small car, but her words floated back, still coated with laughter. 'Kisses don't make babies. You're safe, mate.'

Safe?

Safe?

Who was she trying to kid?

Mac wasn't in a remotely safe place right now. What was worse, a part of him didn't think he wanted to be either. The part that wanted to go after Julia right now and grab her and take her in his arms for another kiss.

At least part of his head was still functioning sensibly. He wrenched open the heavy door of his vehicle, eager to shut himself into the temporary sanctuary.

'He *what*?'

'Kissed me. Come on, Annie. This line is so good you might as well be here sitting on the end of my bed. You heard just fine.'

'I'm just...surprised.'

'You and me both.' Julia's laugh was hollow. 'Actually, I have the horrible feeling it might have been me, kissing *him*.'

'Who made the first move?'

'Him. No, me. Oh, God, I don't know. I was worried about him after the job because he'd been so quiet and I kind of ambushed him in the car park. And…and it just kind of happened. The thing is, what am I going to do about it?'

'Why do you have to do anything about it?'

'Because he's my partner. The last three months have been the best I've ever had and I don't want to spoil our working relationship. I might have already!'

'Why? Was it a horrible kiss?'

'No…' Julia's sigh was heartfelt. 'It was even better than I thought it would be.'

'A*ha*!' Her sister pounced. 'I knew you fancied him.'

'Of course I fancy him. Who wouldn't? He's gorgeous.'

'So what's the problem? You're a big girl now, Jules. Go for it. Lord knows, a fling would do you the world of good. How long has it been? Two years?'

'Nearly three.'

'So this is the perfect opportunity.'

'Why?'

'You've only got another three months there. More than long enough to find out if it's a real possibility. An easy way out if it's not. Life shouldn't be all work and no play, you know.'

'That's rich, coming from you.' Julia chuckled. Then she sighed. 'It wouldn't be just playing,' she said then. 'And that's why I can't go there. It's just too scary.'

There was a short silence on the other end of the line. 'You wouldn't say that unless there's something really special about him. You think you're going to fall in love with him and get hurt again, don't you?'

'I'm probably halfway there already,' Julia groaned. 'And if I wasn't before that kiss I certainly am now.'

'All the more reason to try it out.'

'*I can't.*' Julia shook her head even though her sister was half a world away from seeing the decisive action. 'No way. Because he's special. One of us would end up getting hurt. Probably me. Maybe both of us.'

'Not necessarily.'

Julia spoke softly. 'He adores kids, Anne. He's the perfect father-in-waiting.'

'Oh-h-h…'

The sound was so full of understanding and sympathy it brought tears to Julia's eyes.

'You won't believe what I said to him after that kiss.'

'What?'

'I said…' Julia had to catch her breath to swallow a sob that was determined to escape. 'I said that he'd have to marry me now because of what Sister Therese used to say at school. Do you remember? About kissing and babies?'

'Oh, no!' But Anne was laughing. 'Why do you do it to yourself, hon? Every time. Salt in wounds and all that.'

'It's the way I deal with stuff. You know that.'

Her sister's voice was soft. 'I know you're not as tough as you like to make out, Jules. I know how much it can hurt.'

'Better to make jokes than let people feel sorry for me. Or not to tell them and let things go further than is good for anyone involved.'

'Mac's not Peter.'

'No. I doubt there's anyone on earth that quite matches my ex-fiancé in the creep stakes.'

'It's been three years. Maybe it's time to have a look and see what else is out there. When was the last time you met anyone you were attracted to this much?'

'Three years.' Julia gave an unamused huff. 'Tell you what, if I come across any nice widowers with a few motherless children in tow, I'll pounce, I promise.'

'There are plenty of men who could actually handle adoption. Or surrogacy.'

'Or who would *say* they can. Where have I heard that before?' Julia couldn't help the bitter edge to her voice. 'And then they'll turn up two weeks before the wedding and say, "Oops, sorry, babe. I got someone else pregnant and guess what? It is a major after all."' Neither could she help the spill of words she'd kept bottled up for so long. '"I didn't realise how amazing being a father was going to be and this is the *real* thing. I didn't have to go into some cubicle in a clinic and look at dirty magazines and—"' Julia stopped abruptly, gave a huge sniff and then cleared her throat. 'Sorry,' she added quietly.

'Don't be. You should have said all this a long time ago instead of brushing it off and putting on such a brave front.'

'I guess I've been thinking about it all again, thanks to that kiss. No, actually…' Julia closed her eyes. 'I've been thinking about it since the first day on the job here. Since I saw who I'd be working with. I've thought about it every time I've seen him with kids. The way he is with them.'

She didn't notice the way her tone softened. 'He's a born dad. You should have seen him today. We had this little girl on the train. Carla, her name was. She was only seven and *so* scared and then I handed her up to Mac and he just has to look at her and she's *smiling*. It was—'

'Hey, I think I saw that on the news when I walked past someone's television this morning,' Anne interrupted. 'I haven't had time to check the papers. I knew it was in the UK somewhere but I didn't realise you were involved.'

'Yep. It was up between Edinburgh and Inverness. Bang in our patch.'

'I saw someone dangling off the bridge trying to look in the windows of the carriage. It looked horrific. Was that Mac?'

Julia remembered hearing a helicopter hovering that could well have contained a news crew. 'It was probably me,' she admitted. 'I went down first to assess things.'

'Oh, my God!' Anne groaned. 'Don't tell me it was you who climbed inside the carriage to get people out. Good grief, you must have. You were just telling me about that little girl.'

'Someone had to,' Julia said matter-of-factly. 'And it's what I do, remember?'

'How can I forget?' Julia heard a heavy sigh. 'I want you home safe and sound, Jules. The sooner the better, thanks.'

'Stop worrying so much.'

'It's what *I* do, remember? I'm your big sister. I...miss you, kiddo.'

'I miss you, too.'

Oh, dear. This conversation was supposed to

be picking her up after a miserable day of work when she hadn't been able to find anything to take her mind off Mac. Or that kiss. Or put a stop to the flashes of desire and hope that always spiralled into hopelessness. Now she was going to be feeling homesick on top of heartsick.

'How are *you*, anyway?' she asked brightly. 'How's work?'

'Flat out,' Anne said co-operatively. 'We had three cases back to back yesterday and they were all complicated. The biggest was an ostium primum atrial septal defect that extended through both AV valves into the ventricular septum.'

'Wow! How did that go?'

'Great. Little Down's syndrome girl. Very cute. She was awake when I did my rounds in PICU this morning.'

Julia swallowed. Was the mere mention of a child enough to drag her thoughts back to yesterday? To Mac?

'Any word on that consultancy position?'

'They're going to advertise it soon. Richards thinks I'll be a top contender.'

'You'll get it. Good heavens, you're going to be a consultant paediatric cardiac surgeon by the time you're thirty-five. Go, you!'

'I'm not holding my breath. I've been working towards this for nearly fifteen years. I can wait as long as it takes.'

'Wait until I get home, anyway. I want to help celebrate.'

'I'll tell them not to advertise for a couple of months, shall I?'

'You do that.' Julia was smiling again but something new was being added to the mix of emotions she'd been grappling with. Three months wasn't very long. She was already half-way through her time here and look how fast it had gone. It would only seem a blink until she was heading home again and then she'd never see Mac again. She'd never know what might have happened if she'd…

'Hey, it's Saturday on your side of the world.' Desperation was providing another distraction.

'You've got a night off for once. You and Dave going out on a hot date?'

'I will if you will.'

Something in her sister's tone made Julia's heart sink. 'Things not going any better, then?'

'Worse if anything,' Anne admitted. 'I get the feeling he wants me to choose between him and my career. He wants a family. How did life get so mixed up?'

'It's crazy, isn't it? You can have kids and don't want any because you've already been a mother to me, and I can't and…' Her voice trailed off. It was the biggest dream of all, wasn't it? A home and family of her own.

It was Anne's turn to try and provide distraction. 'We've got each other,' she said stoutly. 'And we've both got amazing careers. Now, tell me all about this job with the train.'

'It was unreal. It's been all over the Sunday papers here. I'll scan the articles and email them to you.'

'Please. But tell me about it first so I won't have kittens when I see the pictures.'

'OK.' This was good. Anne's career was so much part of her, it was inseparable from who she was. Julia needed to be more like that. So passionate about her career that anything else got at least a slightly lower priority. Things like relationships. That ordinary kind of family unit she'd never had herself as a child and could never create for any children of her own.

She was a survivor. She'd already survived being orphaned as a young child, hadn't she? And a brush with cancer that had led to a hysterectomy at the age of twenty-two, for heaven's sake. Life couldn't throw anything at her that she couldn't handle.

'We got the call about 2 p.m.,' she told her sister. 'And when we spotted the target, I really couldn't believe what I was seeing...'

CHAPTER FOUR

THANK heaven for uniforms!

If she didn't have a uniform to put on, Julia might have had the entire contents of her admittedly meagre wardrobe strewn over her bed this morning, thanks to a bad dose of what could only be described as 'first date' nerves.

She hadn't seen Mac for two days.

Two days of worrying about how it would be when they saw each other for the first time in the wake of *that* kiss.

Two nights of reliving said kiss and her imagination hadn't held back in exploring what might have happened if they'd been somewhere other than an open car park. Or if she hadn't pulled away and then done her best to dismiss the moment by cracking a stupid joke about it.

The night time was manageable. Private. A guilty but irresistible pleasure.

It was the day time workings of her overactive imagination that was causing the nerves. So many scenarios had presented themselves. The worst was an awkward coolness between herself and Mac that everyone would notice and would make working together a misery instead of a joy.

At the other end of the spectrum, she could imagine an escalation of attraction which drew them together like human magnets. And that would probably have exactly the same effect due to the kind of tension it would create.

The best she could hope for was something in the middle. A return to the status quo but with a connection that had been deepened. A step towards a genuine friendship perhaps.

That was what Julia really wanted.

'Who are you trying to kid?' she muttered at her reflection, pausing in disgust as she realised what she was about to do.

In disgust, she threw the mascara wand back

into the drawer. Make-up was an occasional in-
dulgence and only ever used for a night out.
Never for work. What *was* she thinking?

As if she didn't know!

'Focus,' she ordered herself, tucking the black
T-shirt with the red SERT insignia into her black
trousers.

'On your career,' she specified, lacing up her
steel-capped black boots. 'Like Anne does. It's
all you need to do.'

She tied the knots in the laces tightly. 'You're
going to be the best you possibly can be in a job
you absolutely love,' she said aloud.

The determined talk to herself was helpful. It
worked right through the fifteen-minute drive
from the farm cottage she was leasing and got
her through parking close to that big, black vehicle and the stone wall that marked the spot
where the kiss had happened.

The flashback was so powerful she actually
raised her hand to touch her lips, convinced she
could feel the pressure of his all over again.
Impossible not to push that mental rewind button

as she had so many times already. Back to before the kiss had happened. To that delicious *waiting*. Knowing what was about to happen and experiencing a more intense anticipation than she would have believed anything could engender.

Julia tore her gaze away from the wall. She could stop doing this. Stop thinking about it. She couldn't stop that odd kick in her gut, though, or the tingles that shot out from it to spread throughout her entire body but she could—and did—ignore their significance. It was nothing more than a physical thing. She could deal with this.

At least, she could until she walked into the messroom and saw what it was that she *really* wanted, standing there beside the bench, making coffee.

Mac.

Tall. Solid. Julia eyed his back cautiously, hoping like hell he wouldn't turn around until she got her errant mind—and body—back under control.

He's not even that good looking, she thought

somewhat desperately. He's…rugged. His nose and mouth are a bit big and he's got that odd dimple in the middle of his chin. And he looks older than he is. Kind of weathered.

And he's got some other woman he cares about. One with long, blonde hair.

Yes. Maybe this was the track to take. It certainly felt like a splash of cold water. Julia poked her fingers through her own hair, making the spikes more prominent.

A pixie cut, the hairdresser had promised, but it looked more like a hedgehog now that it had grown out a little. Appropriate, really, given her short, little legs.

That blonde woman was probably tall. And beautiful.

And that was fine, because she wasn't interested in Mac as anything other than a colleague.

Oh, Lord. This was going to be every bit as dreadful as she'd feared.That kiss had unleashed something that had to be chained up again. Currently it felt like something far too wild to even begin trying to handle. It was too hard to move her feet and take the first step in any attempt. Her heart was thumping and her stomach was tying itself into a painful knot.

And then Mac turned his head. 'Hey, Jules. Want a coffee?'

It was exactly what he would have said last week. In exactly the same kind of tone. The knot inside began to melt and Julia's heart gave a peculiar kind of wiggle and then settled into a steady rhythm she could ignore. It was going to be OK.

She nodded. 'Yes, please.'

And here it was. The first challenge. Eye contact that would be far too easy to maintain and allow to continue long enough to be significant. To send messages that Julia had no intention of transmitting. But Mac's glance only brushed hers. Just a whisper of contact. The kind you might make with a complete stranger.

It should have been reassuring.

It certainly shouldn't feel like a physical shove

to push her away and even if it did, it shouldn't feel this disappointing.

The Sunday papers were still scattered all over the big table in the kitchen area. Julia made an effort and shifted her focus.

'They took some great pictures, didn't they? I love that one of you and Carla being winched up. You should contact the paper and see if you can get a copy.'

'The TV footage was even better.' Mac came towards her, carrying two steaming mugs. He put one in front of Julia and then sat down. 'They caught you climbing into the carriage. Did you see it?'

'No.' Julia was happy to follow Mac's example and sit down. Maybe she could relax all those tense muscles now because Mac sounded completely normal. As though the kiss had never happened. Her smile was rueful. 'I think my sister did, though. She's planning my obituary in case I don't make it back home.'

Mac smiled. Just one of those crooked, half-smiles he was so good at but Julia was aware of that melting sensation inside again. She reached for her mug and cupped her hands around it as though needing the comfort of its warmth.

'I heard you telling Ken about her. She sounds pretty special.'

Julia risked an upward glance. This was different. A conversation about something personal? But Mac's expression was simply interested. She couldn't read anything more into this step onto new territory.

She shrugged. 'Yeah…probably not the done thing to share one's life history with a patient but he needed distraction.'

Mac was pulling a section of the newspaper closer, signalling that the personal conversation was over, but then Julia was surprised again.

'Not many people get raised by a sibling,' he said.

'No. She's an amazing person.' Julia was happy to talk about this. This was exactly the kind of conversations that colleagues on the way to being friends could have. 'She was only six and I was a baby when Mum died but Dad always said she grew up overnight and turned into a mother instead of a sister. When she wasn't at school she had to be the one looking after me, and woe betide any nanny who tried to interfere.'

Mac raised an eyebrow. 'Determination is a family trait, then?'

'Yeah...' Was that a compliment of some kind? Way too hard to tell and why on earth was she bothered, anyway? She really, really didn't want this kind of emotional roller-coaster going on in her head.

She could ignore it and it would go away. Julia concentrated on her coffee for the short silence that followed. In the normal run of things, they might have a brief conversation but then they'd probably look at the papers while they finished their drinks. Or discuss what the day might bring. There was no one else on station at the moment, which meant the road crews were busy. If there were no callouts for the specialist crews they could be used to help cover other work.

Julia was hoping that the silence was only

feeling awkward for herself but Mac's abrupt question advertised otherwise.

'She's a doctor? Your sister?'

'A paediatric cardiothoracic surgical registrar, no less.'

'That's extremely impressive.'

'Sure is. I'm very proud of her.'

'But you weren't tempted to go to med school yourself?'

'Tempted, yes. But then I thought about being confined in an ED or a theatre or a general practice and I got cabin fever.'

'You wanted adventure.'

'Yeah.'

'A bit of danger.'

'Too right!'

'No two jobs the same.'

'You got it.' They were both smiling now. Of course Mac got it. They shared a passion for this work and it was a connection far too strong to ignore.

We're talking about *work*, Julia reminded herself. *That's* the connection. We're colleagues.

So why did it feel like something else entirely? That rapid-fire exchange seemed to have derailed them both and led them straight back to where they'd been…the moment before that kiss.

Mac's smile faded and he looked away. 'I'm not surprised she worries about you. She's still being a mother, isn't she?'

'Kind of.' Julia sucked in a breath, pushing this man and her reactions to him out of her head. Trying to concentrate and think about her sister, instead. It was a complicated relationship that had undergone a huge change as she'd left her teens. A rough couple of years, those had been, what with the diagnosis of early endometrial cancer, the surgery and the grief that had accompanied her recuperation with such a huge adjustment needed in what she had envisaged as her future. 'She's like a mother and a sister and a best friend all rolled into one, I guess.'

Mac was silent for a heartbeat. 'You must miss her.'

'I do.'

He cleared his throat. 'Guess you'll be looking forward to getting home, then.'

And there it was. Challenge number two. Had Mac intended any significance behind those words? If she said she couldn't wait to get back to the other side of the world, she could ensure that any thoughts he might have of following up on that kiss would be buried because she would really be saying she wasn't interested in him.

The split second of identifying that significance was enough of a hesitation. Mac stood up and took his mug back to the sink to rinse it. The question morphed into a statement and left the clear impression that the fact she was looking forward to leaving was acceptable.

A relief, even?

He could do this.

That pesky part of Mac's brain that was attached to something much lower on his body just needed a bit more squashing and it would fit neatly into a box that could be locked and then ignored.

He'd managed well so far today, apart from that tiny prod he hadn't been able to resist this morning, asking if Julia was looking forward to getting home. Alert for a flicker of something other than the impression she was trying very hard to pretend that kiss had never happened. Testing her. Or testing himself?

Whatever. They had both passed.

They'd tidied and restocked the back of the helicopter and then their kits but all they'd discussed had been things like the strength of disinfectant to use or the fact that they were low on IV supplies and morphine. It hadn't helped that the busy start to the day for the road crew had become an unusually quiet day and, once he and Julia had moved inside to do the kits, they were hanging around, keen to hear as much inside detail as they could about the train-crash scene.

'So how did you tackle the fractured femur?'

'Usual protocol,' Julia responded as she pulled pockets of the back packs open and laid out their contents to see what was missing. 'Oxygen, fluids, pain relief and a traction splint. Just the same as you'd be doing.'

'Bit different, hanging in mid-air with a vertical aisle! Must have been hellishly awkward.'

'Jules can work anywhere,' Mac told them. 'She's like a cross between a contortionist and...'

He had to think of something that could describe both her level of endurance and the way she could use her body. Impossible not to let his gaze rest on that body for a moment as he tried to come up with that word. No overalls right now. She was wearing the team T-shirt and it hugged the curves of her upper body. Her arms were bare and he could see the definition of her muscles. She was as fit as he was. If he touched her upper arm, it would be firm. Those curves on the front of her T-shirt wouldn't be firm, though, would they? They'd be... Oh, *God*! Desire seeped out of that mental box, that wasn't secure enough yet, to tackle him like a solid force. He hurriedly shifted his gaze back to that defined biceps.

'A weightlifter,' he supplied.

Nobody had noticed his hesitation. Julia was wrinkling her nose at him.

'Gee, thanks, mate,' she huffed. 'You make me sound like some kind of muscle-bound circus act.'

Mac grinned. And then quirked an eyebrow, keeping his tone very casual. 'I only meant that you're supple. And strong. It was a compliment.'

'Oh-h-h.' The look Julia gave their audience said that this was a one-off, getting a compliment. The look she flashed in Mac's direction said something rather different. There was almost a question there—as though she was puzzled by something.

That kiss was still there. Hanging in the air between them.

'Not that strong,' she said in a tone as offhand as his had been. 'I couldn't have got her onto that stretcher without you, let alone up and out of the carriage.'

Mac leaned past her to drop a new pack of luer

plugs onto one of the piles. 'We make a good team,' he said. 'That's all.'

There. He'd said it aloud and he could feel the way Julia stilled for a moment. As though she was capturing his words and soaking in their significance. The kiss was history. They were colleagues again. Nothing more.

'What about the other guy?' Mac was grateful for the voice of the paramedic. Moving them on and chasing that moment into the past, where it belonged—along with that unfortunate kiss.

'You mean Ken?' Was he imagining any strain in her voice? 'The one with the spinal injury?'

'Yeah.'

'That *was* tricky,' she said. No. She sounded normal. Delighted to be discussing something professional. 'There was a bit more to worry about than there would have been getting him out of, say, a car crash. We knew we had to get him out of the seat and then up the aisle before we could keep him horizontal.'

'Did you use a KED?'

'Absolutely. Couldn't have managed without one.'

'What level was the lesion?'

'Reasonably high. Paresthesia in both hands.'

'Diaphragmatic breathing?'

'No. And he didn't go into a significant level of neurogenic shock, fortunately.'

Mac was only half listening, vaguely irritated by the chatter without knowing why. He kept himself busy sorting an airway roll and putting endotracheal tubes into order by size, finding the guide wires and bite blocks to put back into their correct slots, but he found himself wishing some road-based pagers would sound.

Finally, they did.

'Priority three,' the paramedic said, clearly disappointed. 'Probably a transfer. If you guys get something good happening while we're out, you'll owe us a beer.'

A vaguely tense silence fell once they were alone in the messroom again. Mac fiddled with the kit, making sure everything was perfectly aligned. He was simply too aware of their proximity, that was all. Too aware that the kiss had changed something. It had been a mistake on both sides and they were both doing their best to pretend it hadn't happened, but it had and now it was just…there.

But they couldn't talk about it. If they did, it would be tantamount to admitting attraction and Mac didn't want that conversation. He didn't want to talk about it. He didn't want to *think* about it because if he did, he couldn't control the pull that came in its wake.

A pull towards something he really didn't want. Territory he was more than content to be exiled from. This pull was stronger than anything he'd come across in ten years of voluntary exile. And for the first time it felt like he was in a place he might not want to be in for much longer.

A lonely place.

He didn't like that feeling. It was a relief when Julia broke the silence.

'Mac?'

He looked up. Hell…there was a plea in her eyes. She wanted something from him and if she asked, it might take more strength than he had to refuse.

'Mmm?' It was a noncommittal sound.

'Do you think…if it stays this quiet…?'

She was hesitant. About to ask for something that might not be entirely professional? Mac's mouth went curiously dry.

'I was hoping…' Julia's smile was mischievous '…that we might be able to sneak out and go and visit Ken.'

Mac was quiet again.

He was driving the late-model SUV that was the SERT team's road vehicle, having checked with Control that it was all right for them to head into the city to visit the hospital Ken had been admitted to. If necessary, they could head for the helipad or any other job at a moment's notice.

This car had only the front seats. The back was packed with all the equipment they could need in an emergency but there was no stretcher. It was used as an advance vehicle to get to a major incident first, an area where no ambulance was available or as back-up for a serious case. An ambulance had to be dispatched as well for transporting any patients and sometimes, if the patient required treatment beyond the skill level of an available road crew, they would have to abandon this vehicle to travel to the hospital and then retrieve it later.

Julia was becoming increasingly aware of how quiet Mac was as she listened in on the radio traffic. The blips advertising a new message were coming thick and fast. An ambulance was being dispatched to a three car pile-up. Someone else was reporting an NFA from another scene. No further assistance was required there because it was a DOA rather than the cardiac arrest that had been called in. A crew patched through advance notice of a critically ill stroke patient they were transporting to a receiving emergency department and a vehicle was being sent to a rural area to be on standby while the fire service dealt with a house fire.

Busy but nothing out of the ordinary. Julia had her fingers crossed that a call wouldn't come in the next little while. Long enough for them to visit Ken and see how he was getting on. And long enough to find out why Mac seemed to have withdrawn again.

Not as much as he had the other night, travelling back from the train crash but enough to worry Julia and chip away at this morning's relief when it had seemed like they could get past any awkward aftermath of that kiss. His message had been received loud and clear. They were a good team and that was all, but they'd never had this odd tension between them before. Silences that became loaded so quickly.

And Mac had made a tentative step towards friendship this morning, hadn't he? She could reciprocate and maybe that would be enough to fix things properly.

'So…' Having made the resolution, Julia impulsively reached out to turn down the volume of the radio. 'Fair's fair, Mac.'

He shot her a wary glance.

'I mean, I'm feeling at a disadvantage now. Like I haven't had *my* turn.'

The look was a frown this time. 'I'm not following you. What have I had that you haven't?'

'Information.'

'Such as?'

'Well, you know a lot more about me than I do about you.'

Mac was staring into the side mirror, watching for an opportunity to change lanes. 'Not that much.'

'Enough,' Julia said firmly.She switched off the tiny voice at the back of her mind that was suggesting she might be making a mistake here. 'It's my turn,' she continued. 'I want to know about you.'

Mac was still concentrating on his driving. He changed lanes twice and then indicated an upcoming turn but Julia was watching his face just as carefully and she saw something in the

softening of his features that suggested her interest might not be unwelcome. That encouragement was more than enough to switch off that
annoying little voice.

'You know heaps,' Mac said. 'How old I am,
where I come from, where I did my training.
How I like my coffee.' He gave her just the hint
of a crooked smile. 'All the important stuff.'

Julia laughed, shaking her head. 'That last
one's going to come back and bite you, mate.
And I'm not talking about work stuff. I'm talking about the kinds of things friends might talk
about. We *are* friends, aren't we?'

Friends. It was such a nice, safe word. She
could definitely detect a lessening of any tension
in the atmosphere now.

'You want to talk about football? Wrestling,
maybe?'

Julia's breath hitched. No, not wrestling.
'That's boy stuff,' she said dismissively. 'I'm
talking family. Like what you know about me.
Brothers, sisters, ex-wives…that sort of thing.'

Oh…God! What on earth had made that come

out? This wasn't the time to diffuse tension by cracking stupid jokes.

Mac looked as startled as she was herself. 'You want to know about my ex-wife?'

Julia swallowed. 'You *have* one?'

A tiny pause and then a huff of sound that had an unmistakably ironic twinge. 'No.'

She had to laugh again, to hide the flash of… what was it, relief? Elation? Something entirely inappropriate, anyway. This was supposed to be a joke. Something light that would make Mac smile.

'That's two,' she told him sternly. 'Any more and I can't promise you'll survive the retribution.'

Mac chuckled. 'OK, shoot. My past history is an open book.'

Was it? Could she ask about the blonde woman?

No. She didn't want to know. It was none of her business because this was about friendship, not romance.

'Brothers?'

'Nope.'

'Sisters?'

'Nope.'

'You're an only child?'

Mac sighed. 'Did you really get your degree with honours?'

Julia ignored the insult. 'I wouldn't have picked it, that's all.'

'Why? Do I seem spoilt? Self-centred and socially insensitive or something?'

'Not at all.' The idea of applying any of those criticisms to Mac was ludicrous. 'I was kind of an only child myself, you know, what with Anne turning into my mother.'

Mac turned off onto another road and Julia saw the sign indicating the route to the Eastern Infirmary—the hospital they were heading for. This conversation would have to end very soon and she hadn't stepped off first base, really. Mac was going all silent again so it was up to her to say something.

'It's just that you're such a people person,' she said carefully. 'You get on so well with everybody and you love kids. I had this picture in my head of you being the oldest in a big family. The big brother, you know?'

Mac turned into the car park. 'I wish,' he said quietly, choosing an empty slot to swing the vehicle into. 'A big family was something I always dreamed of.' He pulled on the hand brake and cut the engine.

Something inside Julia died right along with the engine.

The tiny hope that this could have been something. That they didn't have to bury that kiss and make it go away.

It was something in Mac's tone. A wistfulness that told her a big family was a dream that mattered a lot. Something he hadn't had as a child but he could—and should—be able to realise it as a father.

The road that led further than that kiss could never go in that direction and she owed it to Mac not to let either of them take it further.

Not that he was showing the slightest sign of wanting to but she could have kept hoping and now she wasn't going to. And that was good. Any potential for an emotional ride that could only end in a painful crash was being removed.

'Come on, then.' Julia reached for the door latch. 'Let's go and find Ken.'

Their spinal injury patient from the train carriage was still in the intensive care unit but he was awake and seemed delighted to see his visitors.

'Hey, Jules! You've come to see me.'

'I said I would.' Julia's smile was lighting up her whole face and it wasn't just Ken who was captured by its warmth. Mac had to make an effort to look away and find something else compelling enough to compete with that smile.

'I probably won't need surgery.' Ken sounded tired but quite happy to discuss his treatment with the person who'd played such a big part in his rescue.

'That's fantastic,' Julia said. 'So the doctors are happy with you?'

'So far. They've warned me it's going to be

a long road to any recovery and they said we won't know how bad things will end up being until after the spinal shock wears off, and that can take weeks.'

Julia was nodding, her face sympathetic. Then she glanced up at the wall behind his bed which was plastered with get-well cards.

'So many cards,' she said. 'You're a popular man, Ken. I reckon I'd be lucky to get two if I was lying in that bed.'

'I doubt that.' Ken's tone was admiring. So was the gaze he had fixed on Julia. Mac felt a kind of growl rumbling in his chest. He cleared his throat.

'What was the verdict?' he asked. 'As far as damage?'

'A fracture/dislocation in C6/7 and a fracture in…um…I think it was T8. Does that mean anything?'

Mac smiled. 'Sure does. Any changes in your symptoms in the last couple of days?'

'The pins and needles have gone from my

hands. I've got them in my feet instead but they say that's a good thing.'

'It is,' Julia agreed. 'And the earlier you see an improvement, the more likely things are to end up better than you might expect.'

'Pretty much what my doctor said.' Ken had that slightly awed tone back again. 'You really know your stuff, don't you?'

'I'm still learning.' Julia's gaze flicked to Mac and she smiled.

The smile said that she was learning from him and that she was grateful. It made Mac feel important. Necessary. He had things he could give her, like knowledge and new skills.Not that he hadn't already been doing that but it seemed more significant now. The way everything happening between them did.

The pleasurable pride faded abruptly, however, as Mac realised what that significance was. Julia had just reminded him of his position as her mentor. Of her passion for her career and why she was here.

The sound of their pagers curtailed the visit.

Julia promised to visit again on her next day off and Mac was aware of another unpleasant splash of emotion.

Jealousy?

If it was, it was easily dealt with because Mac also realised that Julia had just handed him exactly what he needed.

The key to be able to lock that box.

It wasn't that the reminder of Christine hadn't been enough to warn him off. This was a bonus. Julia wasn't just a woman whose career was the most important thing to her, he was her senior colleague. Her teacher. In a position of authority. To step over professional boundaries into anything more personal simply wasn't acceptable and his reputation and status in his chosen field of work were everything to him.

This was the key.

He would talk to Julia about spinal injuries on their way to this callout. He would quiz her about spinal oedema and paralytic ileus and the scientific evidence that an early infusion of methyl prednisolone could minimise any on-going damage to the spinal cord.

And when they were at the job they could talk about that patient. Analyse the job on the way home. Anything that would foster professionalism.

Yes. The key was in its slot and Mac was confident that it would turn smoothly.

The danger was over.

CHAPTER FIVE

'Do SEIZURES in the first week after a head injury indicate a risk of future epilepsy?'

'No.'

'Why are they serious, then?'

Julia sat down at the messroom table. 'They can cause hypoxic brain damage.'

'How?'

She opened the paper bag to extract the lunch she had purchased at a nearby noodle house. Hers was a chili chicken mix and Mac had gone for beef and black beans. He was using a fork and she had chopsticks but it wasn't the differences in their meal or implement choices that was bothering her right now. It wasn't even because Joe had taken his lunch out the back somewhere so he could have a chat to his wife on the phone while he ate, thereby depriving Julia of some ordinary, stress-free conversation.

No. What was bothering her was that it had been nearly three days since they'd gone to visit Ken and something had flicked a switch in Mac in the wake of that hospital visit. He'd turned into the mentor from hell. Julia felt like she was either listening to a lecture, taking an exam or demonstrating practical skills to an assessor. He was perfectly friendly and smiling as much as he ever had. He was taking an interest in her training that could only be described as keen and he clearly wanted to help her challenge herself and learn more. He was also very quick to praise anything and everything she did well.

And it was driving her around the bend!

OK, so the kiss had been a mistake. They both knew that. She'd been content that they'd reset the ground rules so that friendship was permissible but somehow, after that visit to Ken, Mac had changed the rules again and she didn't understand why. Julia was becoming increasingly frustrated. No, actually, she was getting seriously annoyed.

He was safe. She wasn't about to ambush

him again and jump his bones. No matter how attractive the prospect, she had dismissed any notion of the fling Anne had advocated, never mind anything with more significance.

So why did she feel like the bad guy here? Like that kiss had liquefied and then formed a glass wall that Mac was determined not to crack. Or look through even. By making it so obvious that he was keeping his distance, he was making things worse.

Instead of being able to forget the kiss and move on, this was making her more and more aware of him. He was probably picking up on that and that was making him feel threatened and retreat further.

A vicious circle.

With an inward sigh, Julia tried to distract herself...yet again.

She opened her cardboard box and sniffed appreciatively. 'Mmm. Good choice, going to the noodle house.' Looking up to see if Mac was enjoying his food, she found he had an eyebrow raised expectantly.

'Oh, for heaven's sake,' she muttered under her breath, snapping the disposable chopsticks apart. 'Fine.' She raised her voice and spoke very quickly. 'Brain damage occurs because a seizure involves maximal brain metabolism and increased muscle metabolism. This consumes oxygen and glucose, which leads to hypoxia. Or they may induce airway obstruction and possibly temporary respiratory arrest, which will also cause hypoxia. A brain deprived of oxygen for too long becomes irreversibly damaged. Can I eat my lunch now, please, sir?'

Something that could have been disappointment or even hurt showed in Mac's face but his gaze slid away from hers instantly. The way it always seemed to now.

'Sure,' he said easily. 'Enjoy.'

They ate in silence for a minute or two. Perversely, Julia wanted Mac to ask her something else. She wanted to hear his voice, even if it meant racking her brains to give him the correct answer to a question or an intelligent response to some information.

Or was it because of the feeling she had done something wrong? Upset him in some way? She had a delicious-looking piece of chicken caught between her chopsticks but hesitated with it in mid-air because she couldn't help glancing across the table at Mac as she hit a mental rewind button to see if she had said or done anything unacceptable so far today.

Mac had just put a generous forkful of noodles into his mouth but one hadn't quite made its destination, hanging from one corner. Julia's gaze was captured. And then Mac put out the tip of his tongue to capture the errant noodle and she was aware of a wave of heat that nearly melted her into a puddle on her chair. It felt like a spark had been dropped into a tinder-dry forest somewhere in her abdomen and it caught with a flash like a small explosion. Heat radiated upwards. She could feel it reach her neck and head for her cheeks.

Her hand must have trembled slightly because she lost the grip on that piece of chicken and it fell and bounced down her overalls, leaving a trail of chilli sauce. Julia made a dive for it, snatching it up and putting it in her mouth, hoping she had reacted so quickly her clumsiness might go unnoticed.

She could feel Mac watching her, however. Could feel the tension making the air she was trying to breathe feel like treacle. Oh, *God*! Had he been watching her watching him lick up that noodle? That vicious circle spun faster. Out of control. This awareness was driving her just as crazy as Mac's determination to be Super-Mentor.

Why couldn't it just go away? If Mac trusted her, it would. A flicker of anger at the hidden insult was generated but confrontation was hardly going to help anything, was it?

'Oops, busted!' The old habit of making a joke to defuse emotional overload was too hard to change. She grinned at Mac. 'I'm a piglet!'

But Mac's smile was tight and Julia felt like an idiot.

Repressed anger grew. She was doing her very best to sort this situation out but Mac wasn't cooperating. At this rate, what had been a perfect partnership would be poisoned. They would end up actually disliking each other. Julia was already feeling the stirring of resentment that could very easily express itself as antagonism. She could feel her own smile freezing and her gaze hardening into a glare.

The sound of their pagers going off should have been a blessing but it only added fuel to the unpleasant emotional mix for Julia. Good grief! The enjoyment of her job was going down the drain and now she couldn't even enjoy her food. Scowling, she pushed her chair back and went to the office to get the details of the job they were being dispatched to, ignoring Mac who was following close behind.

Joe was already in the office, looking at a wall map. 'Police callout,' he told them. 'Incident in a known drug house.'

'Great.' SERT training involved the kind of specialist work that could come from this kind of police operation. Dealing with gunshot wounds or scenes where tear gas or pepper spray might be used. They usually involved people who had no respect for authority and for whom violence was merely a form of communication. Way down on Mac's list of preferences any day. Taking Julia into a job like this was even less appealing.

Working with her at all was losing its appeal.

He had been doing so well since that visit to Ken. So confident he could handle this. And then she'd dropped that damned piece of chicken and stained her overalls and that mental key had shot out of its lock. He had lost control big time.

The fabric of those overalls had become invisible and given him such a clear image of what her breast beneath would look like. His body had supplied what it might feel like to touch it. With his fingers…a soft, slow stroke, maybe. Or with his lips…

The effort it had taken to drag his gaze away had been phenomenal and when he had, it had gone in the wrong direction and collided with hers for just long enough to register the way her pupils had dilated. With alarm, no doubt, because his reaction had hardly been subtle. Her skin had been flushed, too, making her look hotter and more enticing that that spicy sauce she had been throwing around.

'I'm a piglet,' she'd said, with that winning grin, and Mac had tried to smile back but he knew he hadn't been forgiven. The look on her face when she'd scraped her chair back. The way she'd ignored him as she'd stomped off to the office. OK, so he'd slipped his control for a heartbeat. It wasn't going to happen again. It was only a matter of weeks until she packed her bags and disappeared from his life. He wasn't going to risk another slip and give Julia another opportunity to dismiss him like that. She could stop worrying. He was going to. He wasn't even going to worry about the potential for this job to be no place for a woman.

'Come on, then,' he growled. 'Let's go and get it over with.'

It was only a short helicopter ride. They landed in an empty car park between railway lines and the back of a rundown housing estate. Moving to a safe point, Mac was all too aware of how deserted it felt. Dark, blank windows towered menacingly overhead. Tattered plastic bags blew around like tumbleweeds and they walked past a burnt-out car chassis and an off-licence with thick iron bars over its door.

Mac did his best to ignore it but every instinct was telling him that Julia shouldn't be here. This was professional, not personal, he decided. For the first time they were in a situation where her size and gender were a liability. He had every reason to order her to stay with the police at ground level until this incident was done and dusted. It was part of being a mentor. It had nothing to do with any desire to drag her away and simply keep her safe because he cared about her in an inappropriate way.

Not that she'd co-operate, of course. Even him thinking about the possibility had given Julia time to march right up to the police van and wait expectantly for their briefing.

'It was a neighbour who made the call,' they were informed. 'Sounds of a fight going on and shots were fired. Then there was a lot of screaming. Still is. As soon as we can be sure it's safe to enter and we've found who's doing the screaming, we'll send you guys in.'

Mac eyed Julia, the words forming that would be an order for her to stay put while he went in alone. Except that he could almost see a balloon over his partner's head right now. One that enclosed the words 'I don't think so, mate!' They would end up having an argument in public and that would hardly be professional. Not only that, she might think he was trying to protect her for personal reasons.

The same kind of personal reasons she had just been disgusted with, having caught him staring at the food stain on her chest. Mac stared back at Julia, aware of how frustrating this was. Couldn't she see that her feistiness only generated problems? If she hadn't been waiting for him in that car park, that kiss would never have happened and he wouldn't be struggling to keep the key in that mental box in his head. Or was it his heart? Wherever. It was huge and heavy and dragging him down. And it was more than frustrating. It was infuriating.

Fine, was the silent message he sent back. *Do what you like. If you won't listen to reason, be it on your own head.*

It took a good thirty minutes for police to gain control of the scene. The occupants of the dwelling, who hadn't been at all eager to allow the police inside, were hauled out in handcuffs.They were cursing and spitting as they were dragged past Mac and Julia and into the back of a secure van. A police officer close to Mac was kicked in the shins and shook his head in disgust.

'There's one more up there,' he told Mac. 'Have fun.'

The man lay on a filthy mattress in the corner of a room strewn with empty bottles, overflowing ashtrays, half-empty cans of food and piles of tattered clothing. His features were sharp, his hair long and scraggly and he clearly hadn't washed or shaved for a considerable period of time.

'Here he is.' A police officer wearing a bulletproof vest stared down at the man, who was groaning loudly. He gave him a nudge with the toe of his boot and the man stopped groaning and began shouting obscenities.

'Oi!' The police officer looked unimpressed. 'Mind your manners or I'll send the medics away and we'll just take you downtown. Do you want to get looked at or not?'

'Not by him.' The man spat in Mac's direction and then bared yellowish teeth. 'I'm no poofter. *She* can look at me.' He leered in Julia's direction.

Julia could see the way Mac's features hardened. He wasn't about to be given orders by someone like this. He was on the point of stepping forward and making this situation worse than it needed to be. She didn't need his protection. She didn't want it.

Those flickers of resentment and anger were easy to tap into. He couldn't make her the bad guy and then step in and get all protective.

Damn the man. She didn't need his attitude or his protection. She could look after herself. It was Julia who took the first forward step.

'What's the story?' she asked the police officer.

'Says he's got a pain in his stomach.'

'I *have*,' the man sneered. 'Don't make it sound like I'm lying. Arghh!' He groaned convincingly and clutched his abdomen. 'I think I'm *dying*. Give me something. Hurry up!'

Julia avoided catching Mac's gaze as she took in their surroundings again. Not that she needed to given the track marks she could see on the man's arms but…yes, there were used syringes amongst the debris. This man was very likely to be a drug addict and this could be simply drug-seeking behavior. Mac would be thinking the same thing. He might disapprove of any intention on her part to take the performance too seriously.

But there had been a fight. Shots had been fired. An intrinsic part of this career she had chosen meant that judgment had to be put aside. Nobody could be left in pain or in danger of a condition being left untreated that could endanger their lives.

'Says he got kicked in the gut,' the police officer added. 'There was a fight going on when we got here.'

Another two police officers were collecting weapons they'd found in the apartment. A sawn-off shotgun, knives, knuckle-dusters and ammunition were already in a pile near the door.

'Have you been shot?' Mac's query was crisp. 'Or stabbed?'

'Get lost,' the man told him. 'I'm only gonna talk to *her*.'

'Come on, Jules.' Mac's tone was icy. 'If he's not going to co-operate, we're out of here. It's obviously not life-threatening.'

'Ahh!' the man screamed. 'Ahhh! *Ahhhh*!'

It was certainly a good impression of someone in agony. Julia shot Mac a warning glance. 'Won't hurt to take a look,' she said.

'I'm dying,' the man howled. 'Give me something…*please*, lady…'

'Let me see.' Julia took another step towards the mattress. 'Pull up your shirt.'

There were no marks visible on an emaciated-looking midriff but it would require palpation to check whether there was any guarding or swelling which could indicate internal damage that might explain the man's apparent agony.

Julia crouched. She hadn't even got down to floor level when a skinny hand shot out and wrapped itself around her wrist, pulling her off balance.

'Stop wasting time.' the man spat. 'Give me something *now.*'

The training given to deal with situations exactly like this meant that her reaction was instinctive. She wrenched her arm down sharply, towards the man's thumb, which had to give way. Then she rolled out of reach, coming to her knees and lifting her head just in time to see her assailant's other hand coming out from beneath a puddle of blanket, a blade glinting in his grasp.

All hell broke loose then. Police officers seemed to come from every corner of the room and within seconds the man was disarmed, on his stomach and handcuffed.

One of the police officers smiled somewhat ruefully at Julia. 'Sorry to have wasted your time,' he said. 'Looks like we can deal with this ourselves after all.'

Julia nodded. She was on her feet now but the awareness of how close that had been was kicking in. Her stomach was a tight knot and she felt absurdly close to tears.Turning, she made an effort to give Mac a smile that would disguise her reaction. Hopefully one that would tell him this hadn't been anything she hadn't been ready to handle. But her smile faded instantly.

Mac looked absolutely furious.

'You just had to do it, didn't you? Jump in without bothering to consult me. Without even *considering* the potential danger.'

'I did consider it.' Julia lifted her chin. She'd had to wait for this but she'd known it was coming.

Mac hadn't said a word as they'd marched along the concrete balcony of that tenement block or down flight after flight of graffiti-decorated stairwell.

'NFA,' he'd snapped at Joe, who'd looked bemused and had then sent Julia a 'what the hell happened in there?' look before scrambling to get them airborne again.

A silent flight. An apparent absorption with a recent emergency medicine journal since they'd been back on station. Until the road crew was dispatched and they were alone in the mess-room. Julia had gone to make herself a cup of coffee and had looked at Mac's back where he was sitting at the table and sighed. Her offer to make him a hot drink had finally pulled the stopper from his bottled-up fury.

'I could see he was an addict,' she continued as calmly as she could. 'And the fact that he could be drug seeking was pretty obvious.' She held Mac's gaze. 'So obvious it would have been idiotic to waste time talking about it.'

'No.' Mac's chair scraped on linoleum as he got to his feet. 'I'll tell you what was idiotic, Julia. Getting flattered because he wanted *you* to assess him. Making a unilateral, *idiotic* decision to go along with what *he* wanted.'

Julia? He never called her by her full name. Or spoke to her as if he was disgusted with her performance or—worse—disappointed with her. And he was saying she was an idiot. Her throat tightened painfully.

'Why do you think he was so keen on the idea?' Mac continued relentlessly. 'Because you were young and attractive and he'd do whatever you asked?'

Julia stayed silent. Battling something that felt oddly like grief.

'No.' Mac's breath was expelled in an angry huff. 'It was because you were the weakest link. The person he was most likely to be able to hurt.'

The weakest link? Oh, God! Mac was working

up to telling her he didn't want her on the team any more, wasn't he?

He was overreacting. She'd been in a room with a bunch of armed police officers, for heaven's sake.

As he had so often before in their time of working together, Mac seemed to read her mind but it didn't take any of the heat from his anger.

'What if those cops hadn't been there?' he demanded. 'What if it had just been you and me, on a street corner somewhere?'

She wouldn't have gone anywhere near him, of course. Julia opened her mouth to try and defend herself but Mac wasn't going to let her get a word in.

'You would have been stabbed. Or worse. I would have had to protect you and I could have been taken out as well. We're supposed to be a *team*. We look after each other and we communicate. Is that so difficult to remember?'

She was going to cry. It didn't matter that in any other circumstance she could have sucked this up and stayed in control. Or that crying in front of Mac was the absolute last thing she wanted to do.

He didn't want her on his team any more.

He didn't want *her*.

Oh, *hell*!

She was going to cry.

The anger, which had very little to do with Julia's decision-making on the last job and far more to do with the fact that he hadn't protected her—that she had made it clear she didn't *want* his protection—evaporated.

They stood there, facing each other in the kitchen area of the mess, the room dim now because it was getting late in the day and they hadn't turned on any lights yet. How had they got this close to each other? Had he been trying to intimidate her with his size as well as punishing her with his words?

Whatever. He was close enough and there was still enough light to see the glint of too much moisture in her eyes. Horrified, Mac watched as the glint intensified and a single, fat tear escaped to roll down the side of Julia's nose.

Mac could feel that tear. Melting something inside himself, and he knew exactly what that something was. The lock on that damned box. Things that had been crammed inside started seeping out. Flickers of images like her smile and the way it made him feel. Pride in her courage. The knowledge that he wanted this woman more than he'd ever wanted any woman in his life. He'd give up anything for her. His life, even. And that was extraordinary. Terrifying. Because he'd honestly believed that nobody would ever be able to mess with his head to this degree now he'd finally got over Christine.

'Oh, *God*…' His voice sounded strangled. 'I'm sorry, Jules. I didn't mean—'

'Yes, you did.' Julia sniffed and scrubbed at her face with an impatient gesture. 'And you're right. It was stupid. I let you down and I'm not surprised you don't want to work with me any more.'

'What?' Anger had become dismay. 'When did I say anything of the kind?'

'You didn't have to.' Julia was avoiding his gaze. 'You think me being female is some kind of liability. That you have to protect me or something.' She gulped in a breath that caught somewhere on the way to create a tiny sob.

The sound undid Mac.

'No.' He spoke softly now. 'Don't you see, Jules?' The words were being forced out. He shouldn't be saying them. But he couldn't no more *not* say them than take in another breath. 'It's not that I *have* to protect you so much. It's that I *want* to. Too much.'

Slowly, her gaze lifted. Caught his and held it.

Mac's hands fisted by his sides as a defence against the urge to reach out and pull her into his arms. He tried to smile but could only manage a brief, one-sided twist of his mouth.'It's a bit of a problem,' he confessed. 'It has been ever since that…kiss.'

* * *

She so hadn't expected this. She had watched and waited for days for some sign of acknowledgement of that kiss that wasn't running in the opposite direction as fast as humanly possible. In the wake of his anger this was such a twist that Julia felt the earth tilt beneath her feet.

Was the anger…the *passion* behind his reaction to that scare today about frustration, not disappointment?

'I thought you wanted to forget about that kiss,' she whispered.

'I did.' This time, both sides of Mac's mouth moved but, endearingly, they seemed to go in opposite directions. 'I tried to. It hasn't worked.'

'No.' Julia's agreement was heartfelt. She knew precisely how hard that kiss had been to try and forget.

For a heartbeat, and then two, they stood there in silence again, watching each other. Julia was soaking in something warm. Joyous, even, because that kiss had had the same effect on him as it had had on herself. Awareness sizzled between them and she finally knew that it wasn't just her feeling it. The acknowledgement that it existed was enough to have unleashed it and it seemed to be getting bigger and stronger with every second that ticked past.

'Bit of a problem,' Mac offered. There was something in his eyes that made Julia want to cry again, but for very different reasons. A vulnerability that tore a piece off her heart. For some reason, that scared him and now it was *she* that felt the need to protect.

'Mmm.' Were they leaning closer to each other or was that wishful thinking on her part? 'Maybe it doesn't have to be,' she heard herself saying.

Mac said nothing but she could sense his stillness. He was listening. Hard. Something Anne had said was trying to filter through this awareness of Mac that was filling her mind. Something about a fling doing her a world of good. That this was a perfect opportunity because it had a clearly defined end point.

Yes. That was the key. Mac was still safe. He didn't need to be afraid. Vulnerable.

'Whatever it is that's going on here,' she told Mac, 'it's got a use-by date. It won't be a problem for very long.'

Yes. She could see the realisation that there was a safety net available dawn on Mac's face. He was being offered a choice here. They both knew the attraction was there. They could live with it for a limited period of time. Or they could give up resisting it. Either way, it would be temporary. And Mac had the choice. She was giving him control. Not that she should be going down that track but if it was what Mac wanted…

'The *problem*,' Mac growled finally, 'is resisting it.'

'Mmm.' Yes. They were definitely closer. Somehow—imperceptibly—they had moved within kissing range. The pull was simply too powerful to resist.

'What…um….' It was hard enough to remember to breathe, let alone form a coherent question. Julia tried again. 'What do you think we should do about that?'

'I can't do a thing,' Mac groaned. 'Unless I don't mind getting fired.'

Julia's eyes widened. She hadn't thought about it from that perspective. Maybe she wasn't giving him a choice after all, just making things worse. 'You mean there's something I didn't see in the contract? About partners being...um...'

'It's unwritten,' Mac admitted. 'But it's also unethical.'

'Why?'

'Because I'm supposed to be mentoring you. Teaching you. Coercing you into any other kind of relationship would be seen as an abuse of power.'

'Oh...' Julia pursed her lips thoughtfully. 'What if the coercion came from the less powerful side of the equation?'

Mac blinked slowly on a sigh. 'It would still be unethical.'

'Because it would interfere with doing our job?'

'In a nutshell. Yes. It's doing that already, isn't it? Look at what happened today. I'm not sure how much longer I can keep up the fight. It's killing me.'

'Maybe you don't have to,' Julia said very softly. Whatever part of her head might have spent a considerable amount of time warning her not to go down this track was curiously silent. Gagged, probably, but it wouldn't have made any difference if it had been audible. She wanted this way too much. More than she'd ever wanted anything. 'What if it didn't interfere with our work? If it was something kept strictly to out-of-work hours that nobody else knew about?'

Mac's eyes were drifting closed again as though his lids had become too heavy. Was he stepping into fantasy or praying for strength? Suddenly, they snapped open.

'It could work.' He spoke as softly as Julia had. 'If we really wanted to make it work. What do you want, Jules?'

'The same as you, I hope.'

Their eye contact had locked. They were breathing exactly the same air. So close now they could feel each other's body warmth.

'Really?' Mac's voice had a seductive edge Julia had never heard before. A low, silky rumble that made her toes curl. 'Do you know what that is?'

Julia could feel a tiny smile playing with her lips but she feigned ignorance because she wanted to hear him say it.

'No. What do you want, Mac?'

His response was a sigh of breath against her lips as he finally closed the last distance between them.

'You. I want *you.*'

CHAPTER SIX

'WHY is it so dark in here?'

Julia peeled away from Mac's kiss before he'd had the chance to do anything more than touch her lips with his own. She dived for the light switch in the kitchen area and filled the room with a neon glare that was almost as much of a wrench as losing that touch had been.

Angus bowled into the kitchen part of the mess. 'Joe's fiddling with that blessed helicopter again. He said he didn't want to come inside because there was something weird going on and here you guys are, standing around in the dark. What gives?'

Mac shrugged, moving back to where he'd left his journal on the table. This was crazy, thinking they could have some kind of affair and keep it secret from their colleagues.

'I was making a coffee,' Julia said in a surprisingly steady voice. 'Want one?'

Angus swung his head from Mac's direction to stare at Julia. 'Something's up. Joe's right. There's a weird vibe. And you look…'

'Like hell, I expect. It's been a long day.' Julia seemed intent on pressing the switch on the electric jug. 'Can't wait to get home. How 'bout you, Mac?'

'Ditto.' Suddenly, Mac was enjoying the undercurrent between them. The totally private innuendo. Maybe this *was* crazy but trying to work with Julia for the next ten weeks or so and not doing anything about the way he was feeling would make *him* crazy.

There was no chance of locking anything away now. The lock was gone. Melted by those tears that had shown Mac a whole new side to this astonishing woman.

An unexpectedly vulnerable side.

Maybe it was just a physical thing for her but she wanted him. Out of all the men on this station who would cheerfully kill to be fancied by Julia Bennett, she was picking *him*.

They were both single, consenting adults so why not?

Mac had forgotten what it was like to feel this level of attraction. What sex could be like when there was more to it than simply slaking lust.

No. He sucked in a breath. He'd never felt like this. He remembered their last kiss only too well and just that tiny brush of contact they'd just had had been even more electric. Sex with Julia would be totally new territory.

Dangerous, exciting, totally irresistible territory.

And maybe they could keep it a secret. Angus knew there was something up but he was frowning. He couldn't make sense of whatever he was picking up.

'The last job wasn't much fun,' Mac told him calmly. 'Some low-life pulled a knife on Jules.'

'Hells bells! Are you OK?'

'I'm fine.' Julia smiled at Angus. 'It was

entirely my own fault and Mac told me off. We're sorted. I'll have to let Joe know it's safe to come inside.'

'If you're sure.' Angus seemed to have forgotten Mac. He had stepped closer to Julia and was eyeing her with concern. 'You…um…haven't been crying, have you?'

'As if!' Julia snorted. 'Try and spread that kind of rumour and you're dead meat, Gus.'

Angus grinned and visibly relaxed. 'As long as you're OK. This job throws some curly ones at us sometimes, doesn't it?'

'Mmm.' Julia looked up from spooning coffee to catch Mac's gaze. 'It sure does. Nothing we can't cope with, though, eh, Mac?'

'No.' Mac held her gaze and it felt like a kind of pact. They could make this work.

It would be easy. Fun. More than fun. He was being given an opportunity he would never have again. And if he didn't go along with the affair Julia clearly wanted, he'd be in trouble. He knew only too well how determined she could be to get what she wanted. Look at today's job when she wasn't going to be left behind at a safe point. Working with her would be hell if he tried to back out now so maybe he should just give in gracefully and enjoy the ride.

A half-smile was playing around his lips and he was only half listening to the conversation behind him.

'Dale should be here any minute,' Angus was saying. 'You can get home a bit early if you want. Any plans for tonight?'

'Maybe.' Julia sounded perfectly innocent. 'I'm waiting to see if something comes up.'

Incredulous laughter almost broke from Mac. He managed to strangle it and turn the sound into a cough. Fortunately, Dale arrived on station at precisely the same moment.

They were free to go where they liked and start their time away from work. Mac caught up with Julia as she walked to the car park.

'What comes up?' he muttered. 'You like playing with fire, don't you?'

'I was just testing.' Julia gave him that mischievous grin he was coming to love. 'It worked, didn't it? Angus could tell something was going on and now he just thinks you're mean and I'm a girl.'

She wasn't a girl. She was a woman. The sexiest, most desirable woman in the world. No, there was no going back now. No chance that Mac could turn away from the path he'd stepped onto when he'd confessed his attraction.

'I can be mean,' Mac growled. 'I probably will be, if we don't get the hell out of here to some place we can stop pretending we don't want to rip each other's clothes off.'

He watched the way Julia licked her lips as though they were suddenly dry.

'Your place or mine?'

Julia's place was the obvious choice.

Private. Discreet.

Mac shared an inner-city apartment with Angus and even though they worked opposing shifts and only saw each other on days off, it felt far too close to work and the possibility of being discovered.

That this was going to be a secret liaison added a dimension to both the connection and the excitement and it seemed more than enough to tip Julia's anticipation into nervousness. Or maybe it was because every time she glanced in her rear-view mirror she could see the big, dark shape of Mac's vehicle shadowing hers.

The intention of this journey resonated in every cell of her body. It became harder to concentrate. Hard to take a deep enough breath. By the time she pulled to a halt beside the overgrown hedge surrounding her rented cottage, Julia had decided she must be crazy.

She had to work with this man. What if this was a disaster? If he found her a disappointment in comparison to that mystery blonde? If someone at work did find out and she was sent home in disgrace? Was the risk really worth it?

Then Mac was beside her and she was fumbling with the key to the cottage and his hand closed over hers and just held it.

Calming her. The way his solid strength always calmed any nerves she might have when facing a job. Julia took the first deep breath she had managed in quite some time. Felt his presence and automatically found courage again. Looked up and saw understanding in Mac's eyes. Heard the same kind of unspoken conversation they had become so adept at.

We don't have to do this.

I know.

We won't, if you don't want to.

I do. I want to. Do you?

You know I do.

Nervousness kicked back into anticipation. Aware-ness of Mac's presence ignited into a desire so fierce Julia didn't notice that she rose to stand on tiptoe to meet Mac's lips before his head had completed its dip.

A soft kiss.

A promise.

And then Mac took the key from her hand and unlocked the door.

Something changed the moment the front door of the cottage closed behind them.

Whatever it was between them was unleashed and free to roam.

The heat and urgency in Mac's gaze sent a tremor down Julia's spine. The tiny hallway of her house made him seem so much bigger. His hair was dark and tousled and his eyes darker than she'd ever seen them and so intent there was no hint of a smile on his face. It made him look…dangerous.

This was dangerous.

Never mind any complications with work. She could get hurt. Badly. She could find that any chance of the future she hoped for was destroyed because she'd never find anyone who could make her feel like this again. That was terrifying—the thought that she might be sacrificing future happiness for something that could only be temporary. If it was—and she just knew it would be—totally amazing, it was only going to last a matter of weeks. A brief interlude in her life.

But she'd known it would be dangerous and

facing danger—embracing it, even—was part of who she was.

She could still say no. For a heartbeat, as they stood there, Julia knew instinctively that this was her last opportunity to back out. That Mac would respect that decision.

But then he reached out and touched her face. A soft brush of fingertips on her forehead that trickled down to end up on her lips, and the touch was so gentle, so *caring*, that Julia knew she was in real trouble here.

Past the point of no return.

Falling in love, with nothing to hang onto to try and break that fall, and even if there had been, she wouldn't be able to summon the will-power to save herself. She felt her eyes drift shut and her head tip back as Mac's lips replaced his fingers, softly kissing her lips and then the corner of her mouth. Her jawbone and then the side of her neck where her pulse throbbed and then skipped.

Yes. It was way too late to save herself.

* * *

She looked…perfect.

The last piece of clothing had been peeled away and Julia was small and golden in the soft light of her bedside lamp, the tan of an anti- podean summer still glowing over her entire body.

His hands felt like they might be rough against the silk of her skin. For the first time Mac felt big and…clumsy, almost. Yet every touch… every kiss drew a response that made him feel nothing short of amazing.

She seemed to know exactly where to touch *him*. The right words or sounds to make that had him on the brink of losing control utterly, again and again. Dear God—she *wanted* him. As much as he wanted her.

But he had to hang on. To make this as good as it possibly could be. He had to *be* amazing because it was the only thing good enough for this woman. And he could be, because this was time away from reality. The past didn't exist and didn't need to damage what they had. What had Julia said? This had a 'use-by' date. Yes. It was a blink in a lifetime but it had the potential to give them both a memory they could treasure. Something too good to forget.

Ever.

So he took his time. Milking every sense. Revelling in the sounds of her sighs of pleasure or whimpers of desire. The sight of that smooth, golden skin and what he could read in her eyes. The smell of her hair and her skin and her desire. The taste and the astonishing feel of every part of her body. Yes. He took more time than he ever had. He slowed things down until Julia was begging. For *him*.

Even then, he tried to be gentle. To ease himself into her delicious, tight warmth but she cried out his name and Mac was lost.

He buried himself in paradise and knew he was taking her with him with every stroke.

Her cry of ecstasy could have come from his own soul. Nothing had ever been this good.

Nothing else ever could be.

* * *

How amazing—that something so good could get even better.

Mac couldn't get enough of it. Couldn't get enough of Julia Bennett.

With the frustration of trying to fight the attraction gone, life was just about perfect.

He got to spend every minute of every working day with Julia. The way he had ever since she'd arrived. Except that it was nothing like it had been.

Funnily enough, it was easy to keep up the pretence that nothing had changed. When they were on a job and dealing with patients they were both ultimately professional. On station, the banter might have had a new edge and the way they stole glances at each other might be more significant but nobody seemed to notice. Not even Joe, who spent more time with them than anyone else.

Angus didn't guess but why would he? Mac never spent a whole night away from the apartment so his breakfast dishes still littered the bench and the pile of dirty socks grew in the laundry.

But even with all those working hours and those glorious, stolen evenings, it wasn't enough.

'What's wrong with you?' Mac asked himself, more than once. 'You've got the perfect woman with no strings attached. No excuse not to be the happiest man on earth.'

What else did he want?

A clock that wasn't ticking somewhere in the background, maybe, counting down the weeks and days they had left.

A whole night with Julia, perhaps, so he could hold her in his arms while she slept. Fall asleep himself knowing that when he woke, she would still be there beside him.

Strings?

Possibly. That way, he could eliminate the niggle in the back of his head that kept pace with the growth of this relationship. The fear that his bed, his job—his *life*—might feel too empty when she had gone home.

Not that he was going to think about that. Not yet. If it was formed into coherent thought or, worse, words, there would be no escape. It would change things. And something told him that Julia wouldn't like it and, therefore, it carried the risk of finishing this prematurely. Mac didn't want it to finish. Not while it was this good.

He'd known from the point of recognising his attraction that the potential was there to get in too deep and end up being hurt. It was far too late to do anything about it now and he'd been there before. He could take comfort from the knowledge that he could survive. It was simply a bridge he had no intention of crossing before he was obliged to. There was an element of hope encased in denial. If things continued to get better, maybe Julia wouldn't want to let it go either.

It was possible to float through life.

What truly amazed Julia, however, was that it was also possible to have someone else occupying what seemed like every bit of space in your head and heart and soul. Mac was the first thing she thought of when she woke in the mornings and the last thing on her mind before she drifted off to sleep at night and yet she still had room for everything that used to be important as well. She discovered that the presence of someone you were so much in love with could seep into everything else and make it better.

Like work.

Within the first few days of that amazing step into a relationship, Green Watch was dispatched to a hiker who had fallen and broken her leg badly in hilly, difficult terrain. A mountain search and rescue team had located the woman but they had no doctor available and needed assistance.

The flight had taken them over Loch Ness.

'Watch out for the monster,' Joe said with a chuckle. 'She's down there somewhere.'

'I see her.' Julia grinned. 'Look, Mac—three o'clock.'

He looked and laughed. 'That's the concrete version beside the museum.'

'You should take Jules to see it,' Joe suggested. 'On your next day off.'

'I might just do that.' The tone was offhand. The look Julia received was anything but. 'How far are we from target, Joe?'

'Be there in five.'

The searchers had abseiled into the base of a narrow gully but it was too dangerous to winch into from the helicopter because of the trees and overhanging rock ledges. Thanks to the bird's-eye view, they found an area beside a stream less than a kilometre away. Not big enough to land safely but Joe could get close enough to make it possible to throw the gear out and for Mac and Julia to jump and then run, crouched low enough to keep them safe from the still whirling blades of the chopper.

The adrenaline rush of the dangerous manoeuvre was familiar enough. The fact that Mac caught her hand to keep her running in the crouched position was nothing new either.

It just felt new.

Knowing he cared about her safety on a personal as well as a professional level. The way she had wished he did that day when she had been about to disengage from the safety of the winch line and climb inside that dangling train carriage.

A dream come true.

A fairy-tale.

And that was why it was OK not to tell Mac why this could never be more than a temporary fling. Because it *was* a fairy-tale and reality could destroy it. Like the best tales, this had a beginning and it would have an end. That the end wouldn't be that they lived happily ever after was something Julia was quite prepared to ignore because if she didn't, that would spoil the middle.

She was living in the middle. And loving it.

The fractured femur of the middle-aged female patient in the gully was easy enough to deal with. She needed pain relief and a traction splint to pull the bones into alignment and reduce both the pain level and the amount of internal bleeding. She needed oxygen and fluids to replace the blood already lost and she needed urgent evacuation due to hypothermia, having lain outside overnight. The searchers carried the stretcher back to the area by the stream.

Mac was the winch-operating expert so he was the one to climb into the hovering helicopter to set up the operation. Julia had to catch her breath, blown away by the flash of fear for his safety as he ran, crouched, under blades that would end his life in an instant if something went wrong.

The fear should have been crippling and yet Julia could still tend her patient and reassure her. She drew up a second dose of morphine and topped up the pain relief and then she was aware of the wash of relief at hearing Mac's voice in her helmet as the helicopter hovered at a safe height above them.

'Sending the line down, Jules. You OK?'

'All good. Ready when you are, mate.'

If anything, the only difference their new

connection made to how they worked together professionally was to improve it. Julia wanted Mac to be proud of her. To not only perform at her best but to improve her skills. He had already seen her intubate critically ill patients and perform chest decompressions to save the life of someone with a tension pneumothorax. On a night shift not long after the mountain rescue, Julia had done her first crico-thyroid puncture to save a man in anaphylactic shock. It had gone perfectly because she'd had Mac there right beside her.

And he *was* proud of her. He'd told her so, in the early hours of the following morning, when they'd stolen some time for themselves in her cottage.

And Julia had never been so proud of herself.

She'd had to tell her sister all about it, later that day.

'It was pretty terrifying. I mean, I could palpate the membrane but it was hard to stabilise the thyroid cartilage at the same time as getting the cannula in at just the right angle and putting traction on the plunger at exactly the same time.'

'It's a good feeling, though, isn't it, when you can aspirate air and know you're in the right place?'

'The best feeling in the world. You know, I can understand the thrill you get out of surgery more now.'

'You sound pretty happy with what you're doing.' Anne sounded almost wistful. 'In fact, I don't think I've ever heard you sound as happy as you have in the last few weeks.'

'I am happy. It's not just work. I'm loving all the sightseeing. Mac took me up to the Loch Ness museum last week. And we've been to look at the Burrell collection and Robbie Burns's wee cottage and heard someone playing the bagpipes on the wall of Edinburgh castle. Mac's determined that I get to see the "real Scotland". He says he'll take me to Oban the next time he goes to visit his mum. Apparently she makes the best oatcakes and shortbread in Scotland. And—'

Anne's laughter interrupted the excited flow of words. 'You're certainly packing in as much as you can. It sounds wonderful.'

'It is.' Unbelievably wonderful. Julia shut her eyes for a moment, remembering one of those outings, when they'd wandered around the Burrell collection, hand in hand, admiring fabulous tapestries and old oak furniture and stained-glass windows. How the beauty had seemed somehow outside the bubble created by that connection between herself and Mac. That the real beauty came from the bright colours and astonishing sensations that only happiness could create.

She sighed. 'I can't believe how fast the time is going, though. It's been six weeks already, Annie. Another few weeks and it'll all be over. I have to make the most of it.'

Anne knew the time frame was all about her relationship with Mac. She couldn't miss the note of sadness in Julia's quiet words either.

'Maybe it doesn't have to be.'

The hope those words generated had to be

crushed. 'It has to be, you know that as well as I do. Hey, it was your idea that I get into this, remember? Because it would do me good and it had a time limit.'

'Yes, but I didn't know how happy it was going to make you.' Anne's sigh was audible. 'Do you think Mac feels the same way?'

'He's just as determined to make the most of the time we have. We don't talk about me going home. It's just there…getting closer all the time. Making everything we do together seem, I don't know, more precious, maybe.'

'You'll have to talk about it some time.'

Julia tried to laugh. 'At the airport, probably, when he comes to wave me off. We'll both promise to ring, or email and keep in touch.' Her voice began to trail away. 'But we won't… Don't worry, Annie. I can handle it.'

'I hope so, hon.'

So did Julia but she didn't say so aloud. If she could hide any doubts from her sister, maybe she could also hide them from herself.

CHAPTER SEVEN

'YOU'RE taking Jules *where*?'

'Oban.' Mac did his best to make it sound like it was no big deal. 'To visit my mum.'

Angus exchanged a look with both Dale and Joe, and Mac's heart sank. He hoped Julia wasn't reading more into this invitation than she had let on. Just because he was taking a girl home to meet his family, it didn't have to be an event of major significance. Good grief. His mother had met girls he'd been associated with before, hadn't she? Or maybe she hadn't. Maybe Christine had been the only one he'd taken home. Mac scowled, irritated by the un-wanted association.

'He's a good boy,' Joe offered into the silence. 'Visiting his mum.'

Angus raised his eyebrows in Julia's direction. 'You want to meet Mac's mum, then?'

'It's more a case of it being the other way round.' Mac looked up again from the paperwork he was trying to finish. 'Mum's best friend Doreen's son Lachlan emigrated to New Zealand about thirty years ago. Doreen wants to go and visit her grandchildren and she wants Mum to go with her. I think she'd love it but she's too set in her ways. Meeting Jules might be just the push she needs.'

Julia was smiling. 'Besides, Mac says his mum's house is a slice of "real Scotland" and I can't go home without tasting her oatcakes.'

'Oh…' Angus was distracted now. 'That's right. It's not long to go now, is it?'

'Just under three weeks.' There was an edge to Julia's voice that Mac could feel like a noose tightening around his neck. Time was running out.

At least the others on station weren't reading anything into the revelation they would be spending some time off together. They were all too busy being subdued at the thought of Julia leaving.

Two days later, Mac collected Julia a little after 8 a.m. He drove them north of Glasgow until they reached Crianlarich and then took the road to Oban. Being midweek, the roads were nice and quiet. It was raining but the scenery was beautiful and they knew each other so well now that they could be together in silence and be totally content. On some of the straight stretches, Mac could keep just one hand on the steering-wheel and hold Julia's with the other.

The periods of silence were not uncomfortable but it occurred to Mac that they'd been happening more often lately. As though they each had things on their minds that they didn't want to share. A discomforting thought.

'Won't be too much longer,' he said.

He could swear he felt Julia flinch. As though she'd been miles away and his words had brought her back to reality with a crunch. And then she blinked and nodded, smiling.

'What time is your mum expecting us?'

'Whenever we turn up. She's only expecting me. You're a surprise, but don't worry. She'll be thrilled.'

'She might not be. What if she feels she needs to give us lunch or something? Shall we take some food?'

'We won't stay that long. Mum can talk the hind leg off a donkey. You'll be exhausted by the time we've been there long enough for a cup of tea, and Mum's always got something in the tin for visitors.'

'Is there much to see in Oban?'

Mac smiled. So she didn't want this time together to finish too soon? That was good. Just as well, given the arrangements he'd made a few days ago in the wake of Julia's enthusiasm for the idea.

'We've got somewhere else to go,' he told her. 'Something I want you to see.'

'Oh? What?'

Mac's smile broadened. 'It's a surprise.'

* * *

Mac's mother lived in a tiny, terraced brick house in an old cobbled street. She was grey-haired, wiry and stern looking, and right now she was almost flapping her apron in consternation.

'Tch! You know better than this, Alan MacCulloch,' she chided. 'Bringing a visitor without letting me know. I'm all topsy-turvy in here. It's a terrible mess. *I'm* a mess…'

The accent was strong enough to make it difficult for Julia to catch all the words but the tone was unmistakable and Julia turned, ready to give Mac an 'I told you so' look. But she saw amusement in his face and the kind of tolerance that only came from a mixture of real respect and deep affection. She watched as he caught his mother's hand and stopped her patting the firm-looking waves of her permed hair.

'Your house is never a mess, Mum, and it wouldn't matter if it was. It's you I brought Julia to see, not your house.'

'Och!' Jean MacCulloch shot Julia an oddly shy glance but she was hanging onto her son's hand now and beamed up at him. 'Look at you, lad… Will you ever stop growing?'

'I think you're shrinking.' Mac hugged his mother, lifting her effortlessly off her feet. She emitted a muted shriek.

'Put me down,' she commanded. 'You're not too old for the wooden spoon, you know.'

'That threat stopped being effective when I was about five. You've never used a wooden spoon on me in my life.' Mac laughed but set her down gently. 'Mum, this is my friend Julia.'

Julia met another curious glance from behind wire-rimmed spectacles. 'I'm pleased to meet you, Mrs MacCulloch.'

'Och, call me Jeannie. Everybody does. And where have you come from, Julia?'

'New Zealand.'

Mac's mother blinked, looking flustered. 'That's a very long way away. Good gracious…'

'Julia's working with me for a while, Mum. We've only come from Glasgow today. We're sightseeing.'

'Is that right? New Zealand... Doreen's Lachlan says it's a bonny place. I'm...thinking of making a visit myself one day.'

Mac's lips twitched. 'Are you going to put the kettle on, Mum, or shall we just stand on the doorstep?'

The house was anything but a mess. Mac insisted on busying himself in the kitchen making tea and Jean insisted on giving Julia a tour of her home. It was obvious that everything was dusted and polished to within an inch of its life. Doilies were positioned precisely and most were beneath framed photographs.

'That's my Donald,' Jean told Julia proudly. 'Mac's father.'

The photograph, in pride of place on a bedside table, was of a man who was an older version of Mac. Even more rugged and more serious but Julia could see that his face would crease in exactly the same way if he smiled.

Jean touched the frame in an action that looked so automatic it was unconscious. 'It's been fifteen years,' she said softly, 'but I still miss him.'

Julia's smile went deeper than merely sympathy. Jean would see that image when she woke in the mornings and before she turned her light off at night. Julia knew what it was like to love someone like that. How lucky were Mac's parents to have had so many years together? To have had a family. Jean looked up and caught Julia's gaze and for a moment the two women just stood there, perfectly in tune. Disturbingly so. Julia had the impression that Jean had her son's ability to read her mind occasionally and knew exactly what she was thinking.

'Come and see Alan's room,' the older woman directed gently.

It was an odd mixture of a guest bedroom and a child's room. Rows of toys and books adorned shelves. Boys' adventure stories, Julia noticed. She'd have to tease Mac about that later. There were old, well-loved wooden building blocks, a tiny microscope, cowboy and Indian models and a train set. Nothing had even a speck of dust on it.

'It's not really his room,' Jean confessed. 'I only came here from the farm after I lost my Donald and that was after Alan had gone away to university. I keep it nice for when he comes to stay and…I keep his toys, of course…for the grandchildren.'

She beamed at Julia but it was suddenly very hard to smile back.

Oh…Lord! She had caught the vibe of her thinking about how much she loved Mac and it was patently obvious where her thoughts had moved onto. What would Mac think if he knew what was happening upstairs? She had been so convinced that Angus had been wrong in assuming there was a deeper significance in this visit.

What was the surprise Mac had talked about?

A trickle of apprehension whispered down her spine. Was it possible Mac was planning to ask her to stay longer in Scotland? To propose marriage, even?

She couldn't let that happen. She didn't want to reject him. She didn't want to hurt anybody.

Including his mother.

So she kept up a bright conversation over the late-morning tea. She told Jean how beautiful her country was and how much she loved it. Maybe she was a bit too enthusiastic but there was an element of panic in there somewhere and maybe if she reminded Mac of how much she loved her home, he wouldn't think of asking anything that might interfere with her return.

She praised the oatcakes and shortbread sincerely but Jean just flapped her hand at her guest. 'They're nothing. I'll give you the recipe, pet.'

Finally, they could take their leave and Julia could escape the tentacles trying to wind themselves around her heart. The solid love Mac's parents had had for each other. That row of toys waiting for a new generation to play with them.

'I think you won her over,' Mac said as they climbed back into his car.

'Oh?' Julia hadn't been trying to win anything. She certainly didn't want to have left Jean with expectations that could only be crushed.

'You sold her on New Zealand. Doreen's going to be very happy.'

'Hey, no problem. Happy to help.' Relieved by Mac's cheerful smile, she grinned back at him. 'Do I get to know where we're going now?'

'Nope. Wait and see.'

So she waited, through a delicious lunch of fish and chips near the wharf and then in the car in a queue to get on the ferry to the island of Mull. A short voyage on a calm sea with seagulls circling overhead, their lonely cries a poignant soundtrack.

When they drove off the ferry, Mac took a turn away from the road to the main township of Tobermory.

'Wasn't he a womble?' Julia's spirits were lifting. This was new and beautiful and she was alone with the man she loved. She'd been wrong to read too much into this and she could relax and simply go with the flow and enjoy herself.

Mac smiled but said nothing. He was, in fact, rather worryingly quiet for the whole drive that took them to the very end of the island where they found a narrow stretch of sea and another ferry.

'We have to leave the car here,' he told Julia. 'No vehicles are allowed on Iona.'

It was well into the afternoon now and the sign stated that the next trip would be the last crossing for the day. Julia looked over her shoulder at the car and then raised her eyebrows at Mac. 'How will we get back?' she asked.

'There'll be another ferry in the morning.'

'But…'

'I've booked a room in a guest house. Upstairs overlooking the beach where we'll be able to smell the sea and hear the waves. That's the surprise. A night in a place where magic happens.'

'But I haven't brought anything! Not even pyjamas.'

For a long, long moment Mac looked down at her, his face so serious that Julia's heart stopped for a beat. And then his face softened and he drew her into his arms and bent to place a slow, tender kiss on her lips. 'You won't need them, hinny, trust me.'

A place where magic happened.

Had it begun even before they'd reached their destination?

Mac hadn't intended anything significant by this surprise he'd planned for Julia. He'd been here once before, as a child, and remembered being overawed by the sense of history, not to mention the sheer number of royal gravesites. The serenity of this isolated little island had stayed with him as well and it was like a cultural jewel. One that he wanted to gift to Julia so she could take it home with her and keep it for ever.

When did that plan start to become something else?

Had it been when he had hugged his mother

in farewell and she had whispered in his ear, 'Don't let this one go, Alan. She's special.'

He knew Julia was special. But he also knew that she saw their relationship as simply a bonus extension of her overseas training experience. A secret one.

How could he prevent her from going?

By asking her to marry him?

The very thought was shocking enough to keep him quiet on the rest of their journey. Thinking hard. Confused by the strength of his feelings. Arguing with himself.

She didn't know him well enough. Or, rather, she didn't know all of him. And there were parts of Julia he knew weren't being shared. They hadn't had time. Or maybe they just hadn't wanted to take that final step into the kind of intimacy that could lead to permanence.

She wouldn't want to.

He wouldn't want to.

Or would he? Faced with the alternative of seeing her vanish from his life for ever, it seemed like a lifeline.

Julia didn't know it yet, but this was going to be the first whole night they would spend together. No going home to the apartment to make sure nobody guessed where Mac was spending so much of his time away from work. Would it be enough to chase away that niggle of discontent for Mac? Would it be enough?

Yes. The magic had begun. Things seemed to be falling into place. Or they would, if Mac could stop fighting it. The serenity of Iona was exactly what he needed. The magic.

They explored the abbey and the cemetery, cuddling together to break the bite of a chilly wind from the sea.

They ate wonderful, home-cooked food in the guest house for their dinner and then he opened the window a little in their bedroom so they could hear the rhythm of the sea as they made love.

They knew each other's bodies so well now. It was so easy to kindle passion. To take infinite delight in each touch…each kiss…knowing what depth of fulfilment they were heading inevitably towards.

There was something different about this night, however. Something that touched Mac so deeply it made him want to close his arms around Julia and never let her go. For this one night, he didn't have to.

He couldn't sleep. He listened to the waves and the sound of Julia's soft, even breaths. And he listened, at last, to what his heart was telling him.

His mother was right. He couldn't let her go willingly.

Maybe he didn't have a ring or anything very fancy to say to her but he could tell her that he loved her.

He could ask her to spend the rest of her life with him.

This was a magic place.

Some of that magic might rub off on them and Julia would tell him she felt the same way.

He'd ask her to marry him.

And she'd say *yes*.

* * *

Sometimes, in the movies, they slowed down the inevitable crash scene.

Frame by frame, you could see it coming.

That was exactly how Julia was feeling, sitting on a smooth boulder on a tiny beach the next morning.

Ironically, the sun had come out and the day couldn't have been more perfect. The sea was so smooth Mac was skipping stones just beyond the baby waves that rolled gently onto the shingle, and she knew it was coming.

The declaration.

The proposal.

There had been something very different about last night. As if they'd been swept along by the magic of this tiny island and it had taken them to a new level in their relationship. The lovemaking had been so intense. So heartbreakingly tender.

Julia had woken knowing it would never be like that again.

The crash was coming.

She had seen it, the instant she had opened

her eyes to find Mac looking at her. The way he had been watching her when he'd thought she wouldn't notice, drying herself after her shower and helping herself to the buffet breakfast in the dining room of the guest house. The way he had almost begun to say something, more than once, but had then stopped himself—as though he couldn't find quite the right words or it wasn't quite the right time or place.

Yes. The crash was coming and it would be her heart—and Mac's—that lay in pieces afterwards.

Her body seemed to be almost absorbing the lump of rock she was sitting on. Something heavy and horrible was taking up residence behind her ribs and it got bigger as Mac turned his head, a triumphant grin on his face.

'Did you see that? Seven!'

'Fantastic. You're the best, Mac.'

'I could only ever do three when I was a kid. I thought my dad was the best 'cos he could do six.'

Funny how you could still smile even when

you could actually feel a crack appearing in your heart. Julia could see the little boy Mac so clearly. On this beach with his father. Skipping stones on a clear, sunny morning.

She could see him standing here again. With *his* son. Teaching him. A little boy who would think he was the best because he could skip a stone seven times.

The ferry was almost due to take them back to Mull. She could see it over the short stretch of water. A new group of visitors was on board, eager to come and explore this idyllic spot. The pilot had unhooked the rope and he threw it onto the boat and then jumped after it. The small vessel drifted for a few seconds and then she heard the engine catch—the loudest sound they had heard since they had arrived on Iona.

A call to action. She watched in dismay as Mac turned from the sea and walked towards her rock. He looked impossibly gorgeous. Faded denim jeans and his beloved leather jacket over a T-shirt. He hadn't shaved that morning be-cause he hadn't bothered bringing a razor and the shadow on his jaw only made him look a bit more rugged. Absolutely…perfect.

The love she felt for this man squeezed her heart hard enough to be painful. To feel like there was no blood left to keep her alive.

The smile of success was still playing with Mac's face but he had a very intent look in his eyes.

One that looked like…hope?

Oh, God! Julia jumped to her feet, propelled by a stab of panic that she did her best to disguise with a smile.

'Ferry's coming. See?'

The observation was completely redundant but she had to say something. Something mundane. A futile attempt at creating some kind of buffer, perhaps.

This was it.

His last chance before they had to leave the magic of Iona.

Surely he was imagining the impression that Julia was fleeing?

He hadn't imagined her response to him last night. At the end, when he'd kissed away the tears of an emotion too great to put into words. When he'd simply held her as she'd slid into sleep, saying nothing because he felt the same way and words could only have diminished it.

But now, on a public beach, when words were all he had, she was running away from him.

Well, walking fast anyway, and there was no reason for it. The little beach was right beside the jetty. That was why he'd been skipping stones with his dad all those years ago because they, too, had been waiting for the boat.

Why on earth had he wasted time with that little excursion down memory lane? Looking into the past when it was his future he should have been doing something about?

Why had he held back this morning, when he had watched Julia open her eyes to a new day and he could have made it the first day of the rest of their lives together?

Because he knew that despite the magic of this place, it wasn't right somehow. That trying to keep Julia might be like caging a wild spirit. That even showing her the cage might destroy whatever time they had left and this morning had been too perfect to tarnish.

He hadn't felt this torn since…

No. He wasn't going to do that. He wasn't going to let any memory of Christine intrude. This was about Julia. About now.

Mac caught her hand and held it as they watched the boat come alongside the jetty. Several young children were hanging onto the rail, shrieking with excitement as the boat bumped against a wooden pile.

He smiled. 'Sound like seagulls, don't they?'

'Yeah…'

Something in her tone jarred Mac. Made him pause and wonder what it was. Disapproval? OK, the children were being noisy and it disrupted the serenity of this spot but they were just happy. Excited. Mac watched a little girl bouncing up and down, unable to contain herself, but from the corner of his eye he could see

that Julia was looking over her shoulder. Back
at the sheep on the rise of a windswept slope.

A last look at Iona?

Or an aversion to the sight of boisterous
children?

'The noise doesn't bother you,' he said quietly,
'when they're your own.'

Her gaze flew to meet his and there was no
mistaking the way her pupils dilated with what
looked absurdly like fear. Horror, even.

'Kids? *Me?*' Her gaze flicked away and she
made an odd sound that morphed into a hollow
chuckle. 'Not in this lifetime, mate.'

That jarring sensation returned as something
rather more solid. He was up against a warning
sign, maybe. Or a wall. The kind you might find
if you'd taken a wrong turn and discovered a
dead end.

He kept his tone light. 'You sound very sure
about that.'

'Oh, I am.' Julia wriggled in a kind of theatrical
shudder. 'Kids ruin your career and your bank
balance and your social life—not to mention

your looks—in one fell swoop. Dangerous little critters.'

Her looks? Since when had Julia Bennett been bothered about her looks? Most women would have had a fit at the thought of being without any make-up or beauty products having being presented with an unexpected overnight stay in the company of a lover. It hadn't even occurred to Julia to worry about anything other than pyjamas.

Something didn't ring true but Mac wasn't about to try and find out what it was. He was too busy coping with something happening in his head that vaguely resembled a train crash.

The echo was uncanny. This could have been Christine talking. No chance of preventing her intrusion now. Her voice was there—loud and clear.

You think I want a kid? Holding me back? Interfering with everything I want to do with my life?

He had taken a wrong turn. Reached a dead end.

Again.

He'd fallen in love with someone who had no desire to follow the same path in life. A path that led to a solid, loving partnership. The kind his parents had had. And, yes, children. To turn that partnership into a family. And not just one child because he knew how lonely that could be.

This shouldn't matter. He'd never intended to get to this point when he'd started this fling with Julia. Thinking about marriage. Imagining children, for heaven's sake. Little girls as feisty as their mother. Small boys he could teach to skip stones.

Not in this lifetime, mate. The words echoed and took on the ring of an inscription carved in stone. So cold and hard it was contagious. Mac could feel it in his heart. Chilling every cell in his body.

At least this time he might be able to escape without making himself look and feel like a complete failure. Before it got spelt out that there were more important things in life than

the dreams he treasured. Dreams that made him
who he was.

Mac let go of Julia's hand. 'We can get on the
boat now,' he said, knowing his tone would be
as expressionless as his face. 'Let's go home.'

If he'd been quiet and thoughtful on the drive
towards the end of the island of Mull, Mac
was very different on the return journey to
the big ferry that would take them back to the
mainland.

His conversation was as mundane as that
observation Julia had made earlier about the
approaching boat. Safe things. Buffers. They
talked about the scenery and the weather and,
brick by brick, Julia could feel a wall being built
between them.

The *weather*, for heaven's sake.

Julia responded on autopilot. She knew perfectly well what Mac was doing. That he was
upset. And she knew why. It confirmed her sus-
picion that he'd been intending to propose to her.
To offer to share his life with her. She'd also

been equally correct in the assumption she'd passed on to her sister all those weeks ago that Mac saw a family as a vital part of that future. Preferably a big family—the kind he'd never had.

She was busy hating herself for what she'd done. Trying to stave off feeling miserable. Bereft, in fact. If she gave it any head room she would have to deal with a grief she'd thought she'd dealt with a long time ago but it was still there. Waiting.

So she talked about the stupid weather and how lovely it had been earlier that morning but how those gathering clouds did indeed make it look like they could be in for a downpour before they made it back to the city.

They were skittering on conversational ice, with occasional silent patches as they desperately sought something safer. Julia thought they'd found it when they began to talk about what would be the start of their working week tomorrow.

'What kinds of things do you think you might

have missed out on?' Mac asked as they drove onto the big ferry. 'Anything we can try and fit into the next couple of weeks?'

'I've done everything I hoped for,' Julia told him. 'A lot more, in fact.'

'True.' Mac nodded. 'That train crash was one of a kind, that's for sure.'

Julia simply nodded. The bonus of a major incident like that train crash hadn't been what had leapt to her mind. It had been something much more personal. The unexpected twist that falling in love represented.

'You were amazing that day.' Mac had stopped the car but didn't get out. 'I'll make sure I put it all in that report I've got to write.'

Julia nodded again. 'Thanks. I couldn't have done it without you, though. You've been the best, Mac.' She found she was brave enough to meet his gaze for a moment. A plea for forgiveness, perhaps? 'You've taught me so much.'

Like what being in love could actually be like. How it could colour every aspect of your life. Make you try harder and achieve more. Be a better person. How had she ever believed she was in love with Peter? Such a pale comparison to what she felt for this man that it would be easy to wipe it from her memory. But she couldn't afford to do that. Especially not now.

'I've already had a look at the logbooks.' Mac's gaze slid away from hers as he led the way up to the passenger lounge and she hadn't seen any response to her unspoken plea. 'I'll pick out the best to put in the report. One thing did strike me, come to think of it.' He held open the door for Julia. 'An area you might be a bit light on.'

'Oh?'

'Paediatrics.'

Julia walked past him and stopped by the rail on the deck. She turned her face away from the brisk breeze and looked back at the island but she wasn't seeing it.

Mac knew that she knew what he'd been thinking of asking. That what she'd said about not wanting children was a deal breaker. But he wasn't going to say anything about it and neither was she. It was for the best if they could shove this back under a mental rug and pretend it had never happened.

They only had a couple of weeks left and then it would all be over. How hard could it be to just let things run their course? Go back to the way things had been only a day or two ago and make the most of what they had?

Very hard, given that Mac wasn't about to forgive what she'd said. She could tell him the truth but what was the point? She knew what Mac wanted. What he needed, and she couldn't give it to him. Maybe it was kinder to allow him to be angry and to shoulder the blame herself. She deserved this pain because she'd known all along that she shouldn't have used Mac like this.

The only problem was that Julia wasn't at all sure she could carry it off for the hour or two it would take them to get back to Glasgow, never mind the week or two until she packed her bags and left the country.

She had no choice. She straightened her back and turned.

'You're right,' she said. 'I'd better do something about that, hadn't I?' Julia even managed a smile as that crack in her heart widened. 'I'd hate to get a black mark on that report.'

CHAPTER EIGHT

THE clouds that had been gathering as they travelled home became a storm that hit the headlines the next day. There were accidents everywhere, with drivers unable to handle dangerous road conditions and the high winds damaging houses and trees, with some unfortunate people getting in the way of the debris. Roads were closed and the emergency services were inundated with calls.

The helicopter was grounded but Julia and Mac had never been so busy. They sped around the city, going from one job to the next with barely enough time to grab something to eat or drink, let alone talk to each other about anything other than the next job. And that suited Mac just fine because he had nothing he wanted to say. Nothing he could say, anyway, until he'd got his head around all this a bit more. The distance created between them yesterday had grown overnight. It had taken a huge leap when Mac had dropped her home and hadn't stayed. He couldn't. He'd needed time to think.

'Angus has been complaining about the state of the laundry,' was all he said. 'It's high time I caught up on some chores.'

There was a lull in the weather, late in the day and Julia and Mac were dispatched to a rural area. A woman was in labour and she was alone in an isolated farmhouse apart from her three other children. It had been the eldest, an eight-year-old girl, who had made the call for help.

'Mummy's bleeding,' she'd sobbed. 'And I don't know where Daddy's gone. I tried to get to the Kendricks next door but the bridge is all covered with water and…I can't swim and…and I don't know what to do…'

Joe had looked dubious. 'We don't know how long this lull is going to last. It's a good thirty-minute flight. No guarantee we'll be able to evacuate her if we do manage to land.'

'She needs help,' Mac said. 'Just how risky is it?'

Joe shrugged. 'We've been out in worse.'

Not much worse that Mac could remember. The flight was rough. Ten minutes into it and he wasn't surprised Julia was looking pale.

'You OK?' He knew his tone was cool but he couldn't help it. The anger that the perfect woman should present herself and then make it clear that she didn't see any kind of future with him was unbearable. She *knew* how he felt about kids. How important a family was to him.

'I'm fine.' She didn't meet his gaze.

She didn't look fine. They hit a particularly vicious air current and the chopper slewed sideways. Joe swore softly but Mac closed his eyes. It had been his call in the end to scramble this mission. What if he'd put them all in danger?

If he'd put Julia in danger?

The thought was unbearable. Never mind that he was so upset. At some level he knew he was being irrational. It wasn't Julia's fault that she didn't have any ambition to be part of a family. It was simply part of who she was. The courageous, clever woman he'd fallen in love with. He'd put his own life on the line, any day, to ensure her safety. Even now with the anger that was a kind of physical pain.

Her frightened gaze met his. He held it for just a heartbeat. He didn't have to smile, thank goodness. He knew the instant the silent message he was trying to send—that they would be all right—had been received. He saw the way she caught her bottom lip between her teeth as she averted her gaze. The movement of her body as she took a deep breath and…he saw just the corner of a determined, albeit grim smile.

And in that moment of courage that he'd contributed to, Mac realised he'd never had this kind of a connection with any other person. That he'd never find someone else that felt so much like a part of himself. It shouldn't matter a bit that Julia didn't share his dream of having kids but it did. It hurt like hell.

'Target sighted,' he said tersely, minutes later. 'Man, that river's high. And look at the trees in it. I'm not surprised the bridge is washed out.'

'Sooner we're down the better,' Joe muttered. 'I don't like the way this wind is picking up.'

The landing was heavy. A jarring thump.

'Sorry 'bout that,' Joe said. 'Everybody all right?'

The wind shook the aircraft and the rotors howled as they slowed.

'What are our chances of being able to take off again, Joe?'

'Soon?' Joe shook his head. 'Nil.'

Mac nodded. 'Right, then. You may as well make yourself useful, Joe, and help us carry some gear into the house.'

A small girl with curly, red hair met them at the door to the farmhouse. She had two smaller boys clinging to her legs.

'Are you Maggie?' Mac asked.

She nodded, her face tear-streaked and terrified.

Mac crouched down. 'You're a very brave girl,' he told her. 'Can you show us where Mum is?'

Maggie nodded again and tried to move but she was impeded by two sets of small arms. One set belonged to a boy of about five who clung to her waist. The youngest boy was about two years old. A toddler who had a firm grip on her leg.

Mac had his backpack on and another bag in his hands which he handed to Julia. He swung the toddler under one arm and held out his other hand to Maggie. She took it without hesitation, her other hand taking her brother's, and Julia had to swallow past a lump in her throat as she followed the chain of small people attached to Mac. It was so easy for him to win their trust. So natural.

No wonder he was so disappointed with her. He hadn't been able to bring himself to say a single word to her today that hadn't had something to do with a job. Except for asking whether she was OK in that turbulence. And even asking that, he had managed to sound distant. As though it was simply professional concern. As Joe's had been on landing. He'd known she'd been scared, too and his expression had told her she had nothing to worry about, but even then he hadn't been able to bring himself to smile at her. Her heart heavy, she trudged in her partner's wake.

They found the children's mother on the kitchen floor and it was obvious she was in trouble. Gripped by a contraction, she was barely aware of the influx of people. Mac handed the toddler to Joe and bent towards Maggie.

'We're going to take care of your mum,' he said. 'I need you to go with Joe and help look after your brothers. Can you do that?'

Julia was already crouched beside the woman, her hand on her wrist seeking a pulse. She looked up as Maggie nodded and turned away.

'What's your mum's name?' she asked.

'Katherine,' Maggie said, her huge, worried eyes turned towards her mother. 'But Daddy calls her Katie.'

'Katie? Can you hear me?'

The woman's eyes flickered open. She was breathing fast but her respirations were shallow.

'My name's Julia and this is Mac. We're paramedics with a helicopter crew.'

'Thank God you're here... My poor wee Maggie.'

'She's fine. How long have you been in labour, Katie?'

'What's the time?'

'Nearly 4 p.m.'

'Doug went out after lunch. I guess the pain came on not long after.'

'Suddenly?'

'Yes...well, it got a lot worse. I've had backache for days. And then my waters broke.'

'How many weeks are you?'

'Thirty-eight... No, it must be almost thirty-nine.'

'And were your previous deliveries normal?'

'Yes. Nothing like this...'

Julia gave up trying to get a heart rate. The

pulse beneath her fingers was thready and fast. No surprises there. Katie had been in labour for hours. She would have been exhausted even without the fear of being in this situation without medical assistance. And on top of that, she was losing blood. Julia turned to Mac, who was organising their gear. He had an oxygen mask already attached to a cylinder.

'Ten litres per minute,' he told Julia as he bent towards their patient. 'Hi, Katie. I'm Mac. I'm just going to slip this oxygen mask on for you, is that OK?'

He smiled at Katie. The kind of smile Julia had been missing all day. The kind that made a patient, who was exhausted and in pain and probably worried sick about all her children as well as the baby she was about to have, smile back.

'We need an IV and some fluids up.' Julia's voice came out a little more crisply than she had intended.

Mac's smile faded. 'Whatever you need.' His

nod was as crisp as her order as he turned back to the pack of supplies.

The message was clear. Julia was in charge of this job if she was confident she could handle it. Or course she was. This was—or hopefully would be very soon—a paediatric case. She needed the experience.

'I'd like the life pack on and a full set of baseline vitals, thanks,' she told Mac. She turned back to Katie. 'I need to check what's going on below. Is that OK?'

Katie nodded. 'Please...do whatever you have to.' Her face crumpled. 'This wasn't supposed to happen. I was going into hospital tomorrow because the doctor said... Ohhh...it's starting again...'

'Hold my hand,' Mac directed. 'Squeeze as hard as you like.'

Julia was cutting away Katie's clothing. She put a towel down to help soak up the liquid on the floor. A mixture of amniotic fluid and blood but she couldn't see any evidence of meconium staining that could indicate that the danger to the baby's welfare might be getting critical. It was hard to estimate how much blood had been lost. Or why it was happening.

'What did the doctor say, Katie?' she asked as soon as she could see the pain of the contraction begin to fade.

'That I had to get to hospital in good time. Something about my placenta being a bit low.'

Julia's gaze flew to Mac's. A placenta that was too low could start to bleed badly as the cervix dilated and ripped blood vessels. How much worse could this blood loss become before the baby arrived?

Her gloved fingers were searching for information. Delivery was well under way but something felt wrong with the baby's head. It was… Julia's heart sank. 'It's breech,' she told Mac.

Katie stifled another sob. 'The doctor said that if she couldn't be turned this week, I might have to have a Caesarean.'

Mac had just slipped an IV cannula into Katie's forearm. He was holding it in place, waiting to secure it and attach the necessary fluids. Waiting to engage in one of those light-ning-fast silent conversations.

You want me to take over?

I know what to do. I just haven't done it before.

You'll be fine. I'm here. You can do this.

She could. It was helpful that this wasn't Katie's first baby. An episiotomy was prob-ably not necessary, which was good because it wasn't in Julia's scope of practice.

'Katie? I know you're tired, hon, but could you try and give a good push with the next contrac-tion?'

'I'll...try...'

She did. The baby's buttocks came into view and Julia was able to hold the hips and apply gentle traction until the shoulder blades came into view. She rotated the trunk of the baby until the front shoulder was delivered and then turned it in the opposite direction to deliver the other shoulder.

Thirty seconds, she reminded herself, to let the trunk hang and protect the head of the baby.

Longer than you think. Count. Then lift the legs and swing upwards in an arc until you can see the baby's mouth.

Mac was there with the small rubber bulb and nozzle to clear the baby's airway and allow it to start breathing.

Now it was Julia's job to control the delivery of the baby's head to protect it against sudden expansion and expulsion. She slipped her index finger into the tiny mouth and flexed the head.

'*Ohhh…*!' Katie groaned.

Julia could feel the pressure as the contraction built. As gently as she could she eased the baby's head out. And despite Julia's concern for the blood loss, for this moment, there was joy. Amazement.

'It's a wee girl, Katie.' Mac's voice sounded thick. 'She looks a very good weight.'

'Let me see…oh, please… Let me hold her.'

Julia was happy with what she could see. The baby was a good colour and already breathing well. With a nod she allowed Mac's hands to slip between hers and she transferred the precious bundle. He placed the baby on Katie's chest and covered them both with clean, fluffy towels.

Julia clamped and divided the cord and began to massage Katie's abdomen to stimulate another contraction and speed up delivery of the placenta. If that was enough to stop the bleeding, they would be all right until they could transfer their patient to hospital, no matter how long it took.

Darkness fell and the wild weather continued. The bridge was washed away, isolating the farm from any roads. Phone lines were down and the power was off. The SERT helicopter was going nowhere. They were stuck for the night at least and Mac was absolutely loving it.

The old stone farmhouse was solid enough to withstand whatever nature could hurl at it and the tension of any medical crisis was over. Julia had handled everything brilliantly. A difficult birth, the careful monitoring of Katie until the bleeding stopped completely and her blood pressure climbed back to normal limits, and a commendably thorough paediatric assessment of the newborn girl.

'Her name's Fiona, for the birth certificate and paperwork,' Katie told them. 'But we're going to call her Noni.'

'Noni,' the other children chorused from the door, drawn by the sound of a crying baby now the proud recipient of a perfect Apgar score by Julia. 'We want to see Noni.'

'Mummy?' Maggie's face shone. 'You're all better now?'

'I'm fine, darling. Come in, all of you. Come and welcome your new little sister.'

It was Mac's turn to take charge of the scene for a while but he couldn't see any reason to move from the kitchen. It was a vast room, with an Aga, sink and pantry at one end, a well-scrubbed table and half a dozen chairs in the middle and at the other end was an open fire-place, an old, comfortable-looking couch and two armchairs.

With Joe's help, he built up a roaring log

fire to warm the whole room. With Maggie's help to locate linen and pillows, they made a bed for Katie on the couch. She directed them to where the bassinette and supplies of baby clothes were upstairs and then to a high shelf in the pantry where they found candles and kerosene lamps.

Mac felt like the hero of the hour when he made use of their sophisticated radio equipment to make contact with the local police, who managed to locate Katie's husband, Doug. He was at a neighbour's property, having been caught on the wrong side of the river when the water level rose. He was safe and so was the farm truck and the four dogs but he had no way of getting home. He had been beside himself with anxiety but, thanks to modern, satellite technology, the parents of the brand-new baby were able to have a brief conversation. Mac had to stay close to make sure Katie had no problems working the radio. Julia was hovering close to Maggie, who sat in an armchair with her baby sister in her arms. There was no way to avoid hearing both sides of the radio conversation.

'Are you all right, love?'

'I'm fine, Doug. I've had the best care you could imagine. Just as good as it could have been in the hospital, honestly.'

Julia looked up and smiled and Mac smiled back. It was true. She had every right to look proud of herself and he was only too happy to share the moment.

'She's here, Doug,' Katie said brokenly. 'Our wee girl is here at last and…and she's gorgeous.'

'Of course she is. Just like her mother.'

'I wish you were here with us…' Tears were streaming down Katie's face now and Mac saw Julia biting her lip in sympathy.

'I am,' came a gruff voice amidst radio crackle. 'I'm there, Katie. I'm with you. In your heart.'

Such an unexpected thing to hear a staunch farmer say. Mac could hear the love. Could see it as he looked around to find the three older children all sitting as still as mice, listening to their father's voice. He could imagine this room in a day or two with no strangers in here. Maybe the dogs were allowed to lie in front of the fire and Doug would be here with his wife and all these beautiful children.

How could Julia not want something like this in her future? He took the radio from Katie and clipped it back to his belt, carefully avoiding a glance in Julia's direction.

'We'll get this all sorted in the morning,' he promised. 'We'll get your whole family back under the same roof, don't you fret.'

And, in the meantime, they had what amounted to a great substitute family right here.

Joe had clearly been adopted as a grandfather by the two small boys, who both wanted to spend as much time as possible on his knee, listening to stories.

Maggie was the responsible eldest child who was determined to nurse her mother and boss the younger children.

Mac stepped into Doug's shoes to cut and haul firewood to ensure the house was warm.

He made sure doors and windows were securely latched against the weather and followed
Katie's instructions to put a meal on the table
and, later, to get the children into their beds.

Julia was a chameleon. A big sister for Maggie,
encouraging her and helping only when needed.
A medic making sure her patients were com-
fortable and cared for and that all the necessary
paperwork was meticulously filled in. A fun
aunty when it came to face washing and teeth
cleaning and pyjamas for the little boys. Hearing
her laughter mingled with the giggles of small
children was like a slap in the face for Mac.

Even harder to see was the way she was another mother for tiny Fiona.

It was Julia who gently washed the baby on a
mattress of soft towels in front of the fire and
then dressed her in the soft, warm baby clothes
available.

'They were mine,' Maggie said proudly. 'When
I was a wee baby like Noni.'

Julia sat with Katie as she fed the baby and

watched over them both with the same proud smile Mac had shared earlier.

And it was Julia who got up at some ungodly hour from the armchair she was dozing in to pick Fiona up and change her nappy and to sit and cuddle her in the armchair in the hope of giving Katie a little more time to sleep and heal. Joe was asleep on a couch in another room. The children were all tucked up in their own beds upstairs but Mac was in the other armchair close to the fire. He had also woken as the baby had stirred.

'Need a hand?'

'No, we're good. Go back to sleep, Mac.'

It was easy to pretend to be asleep. To tilt his head back so his eyes looked closed in the flickering glow of banked coals in the grate of the fire and the kerosene lamp nearby. It should have been easy to slip back into real sleep given his weariness but Mac soon found what he was watching utterly compelling.

It began with the gentle way Julia was handling the newborn as she changed its nappy and put tiny legs back into the stretchy suit. The soft sound of her voice as she made soothing murmurs. He must be doing a good job of seeming as soundly asleep as Fiona's exhausted mother, Mac decided, because he had the feeling they were both non-existent for Julia right now. Her focus was completely on the baby as she gathered it up in its blanket and sat on the edge of her armchair, rocking the infant in her arms.

The whimpering ceased. The rocking slowed and then Julia simply sat, gazing down at the baby in her arms. Seconds clicked into a minute and then another but Mac was transfixed. Was she waiting to make sure the baby was asleep so that she could put her back in the bassinette? No.

The light might be soft and Mac could only see her profile but the intensity of the expression on Julia's face made something inside Mac tighten so painfully he couldn't breathe.

He watched her hand move, almost in silhouette against the backdrop of the glowing fire. He could see the way her thumb stroked the top of the baby's head. So slowly it seemed to go on for ever and Mac could feel every millimetre of that touch himself.

He could feel the...*longing*. The word came easily, really, because he could feel it himself. Could imagine Julia sitting just like that. Holding *their* child.

He wanted to close his eyes properly now because he felt like he was seeing something he wasn't meant to see.

Something very private.

The real Julia? A part he'd never been allowed close to?

A woman who wanted a baby—a family of her own—as much as he did?

Why did that impression feel like a knife in his chest? So painful he had to move? To open his eyes and wake himself up enough to shift his thoughts as a means of self-protection.

And Julia looked up.

She knew he had been watching her. That he had seen something she had intended to keep hidden.

She didn't look angry. Or guilty. What Mac could see was a confirmation that he *had* seen what he thought he'd seen. A desperate yearning for a child of her own. He could see sadness as well. An apology?

For what?

The knife in his chest twisted a little. She had lied to him. She had told him she didn't want children. What she'd really been saying was that she didn't want *him*. But that was a lie, too. This relationship might have been intended as temporary and fun but it had never been a game. Nobody could have what they had found together without it being real.

Without love.

Mac didn't understand. One word was echoing in his head.

Why?

He must have spoken it aloud because Julia's eyes widened. Her voice came out softly enough not to disturb the baby in her arms.

'Why what?'

'Why did you tell me you didn't want to have children? It's not true, is it?'

He saw her look down at the baby and could see the ripple in her neck as she swallowed. Hard. Then she lifted her gaze.

'It has to be.'

'Why? Because I'm not the man you want to be the father of your children?'

The way her lips moved in a half-smile that wobbled precariously made Mac sit up and lean forward, ready to launch himself close enough to protect and comfort her, but he didn't move yet. He might miss what she had to say and it was important.

Life and death kind of important.

'No,' Julia whispered. 'Exactly the opposite.'

Mac didn't understand. His brow creased as he stared at Julia.

'If I had to search the world to find the perfect man to be the father of my children, it would be you, Mac. Don't ever think otherwise. But it's not going to happen. Ever.'

As if to punctuate her statement, Julia rose and carried the baby back to her bassinette.

Mac rubbed his forehead with his hand. 'I don't understand,' he said quietly.

Julia straightened, her arms now empty. She wrapped them around her body. Her face looked pale. Distraught, almost.

'Can't we just leave it?' she begged. 'What we've had has been wonderful. *You're* wonderful. We've only got a short amount of time left and I've hated the way we've been today. Please, Mac...' She took the tiniest step towards him. 'Couldn't we turn the clock back a few days and be like that and then I'll go home and we'll have something wonderful to remember for the rest of our lives?'

Mac stood up and moved to close the gap between them but Julia didn't stop talking. If anything, her words became more desperate.

'You'll find someone else. Someone who'll think exactly the same way and she'll have your babies and you'll be the perfect father and—'

'No.'

The word was more than an interruption. It was intended to stop the flow of words he didn't want to hear. Mac drew Julia into his arms and was horrified to find she was trembling.

'W-why not?'

'Because I don't want to find someone else.'

'You have to.'

'Why?'

'Because I can't give you what you need, Mac.'

'I need you.'

'You need a family.'

'We can be a family.'

'No, we can't.' Julia pulled away. Her voice was still low but there was a fierce edge to it that could have been anger. 'This was never meant to get this far. We had a "use-by" date, Mac. I'm not in the market for anything else.'

'But…' Mac still didn't understand. 'You want children. You've all but admitted you feel the same way I do about having a family.'

'I can't have children, Mac.' Julia had turned away from him now. 'I had a hysterectomy when

I was twenty-two because of endometrial cancer. There's no way on earth I'm ever going to have a baby of my own.'

Mac couldn't say anything for a moment. He was stunned. Shocked but then…what… relieved? This wasn't about *him*. This was an obstacle that a lot of couples had to deal with. There were ways around it. If this was all that was standing between a future alone or one with Julia, it simply wasn't an issue.

He couldn't help his smile. He opened his mouth to tell her that if she thought it had to be the end of the road she was wrong, but she had turned back. She saw his smile. She probably read what he was thinking in his face.

'Don't say it,' she warned. 'Don't you dare tell me it doesn't matter. That it doesn't make a difference. I've been there and done that and I'm never going to believe anything you think you want to say right now so don't say it.'

'Julia?' A faint voice came from the couch. 'Is everything all right?'

'Everything's fine, Katie.' The tone of Julia's

voice changed markedly but the look Mac received was another clear warning. This discussion was over. 'I'm glad you're awake,' she said, moving towards Katie. 'I want to check your blood pressure and things. Noni will probably need a feed, soon, too.'

Mac sat back in his chair. He closed his eyes but he didn't sleep.

OK. This was the wrong place and time but this discussion was a long way from being over. He knew what he was up against now.

He knew he could win.

CHAPTER NINE

SHE couldn't talk about it.

Not yet.

Not when she could still feel that baby in her arms every time she closed her eyes. Could remember the incredible softness of the down on that tiny head, the baby smell, the fierce protectiveness that came with having sole responsibility—albeit briefly—for such a vulnerable little being.

Julia and Mac had been stood down for twenty-four hours after they had finally been able to evacuate Katie and her family the morning after Noni's birth. Mac had wanted to come home with Julia but she found herself brushing him off in precisely the same way he had brushed her off in the wake of what had turned out to be an unfortunate visit to his mother and the island of Iona.

'I need to sleep,' she had said briskly. 'And wash my hair and clean the house and call my sister. I'll see you tomorrow, Mac. At work.'

Hopefully, it would be as busy as it had been during the storm and preclude any private conversation. She knew they had to talk about it because she owed Mac that much at least.

But not yet.

Not when it hurt this much and when her head and heart were at war with each other. When she was feeling tired and confused and more vulnerable than she'd ever felt in her life before.

There had been some powerful magic going on in that isolated farmhouse last night. A sprinkle of fairy dust that had tipped the balance and turned what could have been a tragedy into a joyous family extension. Some of that dust must have still been in the air when she'd picked up the baby to comfort her in the dead of night.

Magic that had stilled the emotional rollercoaster she'd been on ever since she'd woken that morning on Iona with the premonition of the coming crash. Maybe they'd brought it with them, a coating that was shaking itself free at unexpected moments.

That magic had been well stuck on the beach when they'd been waiting for the ferry. When she'd pushed Mac away as hard as she could to pre-empt the declaration she had known was imminent. Even less in evidence when Mac had chosen to stay away from her that night. Self-loathing had surfaced at that point. Loneliness that she'd brought on herself and deserved. A negative spiral of thoughts that if not wanting children hadn't been such a deal breaker, he would have wanted to talk about it. He would have come and held her in his arms and said the words that had never been spoken.

He would have told her that he loved her.

As a downward swoop of an emotional roller-coaster, the frightening helicopter ride had been a perfect bottom of the dip. She could have died, never having heard those words. Never having told Mac how much *she* loved him.

But then she'd had the challenge of a potentially disastrous medical emergency and the adrenaline rush of success. The joy of hearing a newborn's first cry that had broken a barrier and pulled her into family life. Sharing a meal with young children, supervising bathtime and tucking them into bed.

A roller-coaster. Emotions going from one extreme to another.

And then the moment of utter serenity, holding a sleeping baby. An astonishing stillness that had given her a glimpse into a part of her soul she had been so determined to deny. A part a career—maybe even a marriage—could never hope to fulfil. A part that had the kind of unconditional, absolute love a parent could give a child.

No wonder Mac wanted a family in his future so badly.

Had the yearning been awakened in him long ago as a lonely child himself? Would it get worse for her? Intense enough to take too much joy from life?

It didn't have to. Julia stepped out of the long, hot shower and towelled herself dry. Maybe the real magic had been to realise that she could have taken the newborn Noni home and loved her as her own, no question. Adoption wasn't an issue. She could do that one day. Adopt children as a single mother, if necessary.

'Are you *crazy*?'

The words were muttered aloud as she pulled on a favourite pair of soft leggings and stuffed her feet into fluffy slippers.

Mac had been about to tell her it didn't matter that she couldn't have babies. That they could adopt.

Her heart wanted to rejoice. Her head over-ruled it.

History repeating itself, it said. History that led to heartbreak. And this time it would be worse because she loved Mac *so* much. In a way she had never loved anyone and knew she never would again. She hadn't told him that and maybe that was just as well because she'd told him the truth about herself too late and now it felt as though everything they had together was built on something too insubstantial to last.

Too flimsy to trust.

It was only early afternoon. The early hours of the morning on the other side of the world but that was probably just as well, too. If she rang and talked to Anne she would probably start crying and her sister didn't need to know how bad she was feeling. Her sister might feel responsible, having suggested that an affair with Mac was a good idea. She was dealing with the disintegration of her own relationship in any case and, when you got right down to it, she couldn't really understand where Julia was coming from.

Anne didn't have any yearning for a child. Why would she when she had mothered Julia from when she was only a child herself? When her career had her working with children and sharing the heartache of parents who had to deal with the dark side of loving their little ones so much? How ironic was it that they were both in relationships where they couldn't give the man they loved what he wanted but for such different reasons?

Things needed to be done and Julia tried hard to distract herself but the housework didn't take much time and the phone calls and email that were waiting for attention were dealt with just as quickly. Sitting around feeling sorry for herself was stupid so Julia pulled on a woolly hat, padded anorak and rubber boots and headed out into the remnants of yesterday's storm, hoping that a blast of damp arctic air might do something to clear her head. She walked for an hour or more, until her fingers and toes and nose were frozen and all she wanted was another hot shower and to tumble into bed and sleep.

Returning to her cottage the back way across farmland, she missed the big black vehicle parked out the front. It was a shock to find Mac standing on her front porch. He looked as exhausted as she felt. Physically and emotionally. His smile was so brief it almost didn't happen. He hadn't shaved. There was a dark shadow on his jaw line and even darker shadows in his eyes. He looked rugged and unhappy and…so heartstoppingly gorgeous Julia couldn't speak. She could hardly draw a breath.

'We need to talk, Jules.'

Julia nodded. Raindrops trapped in her eyelashes were dislodged by the movement and fell onto her cheeks, like tears.

'You'd better come in, then.'

'You're soaked.'

'I'll leave my outside stuff here.' She shrugged off the anorak and hung it up to drip on the flagged area of the porch.

'Where have you been?'

'I just went for a walk. I needed some fresh air.' Julia was pulling off her boots but she glanced up to catch Mac's wry smile.

'Nothing stops you, does it? I reckon you'd go for a walk in a hurricane if you felt the need for some fresh air.'

Julia's smile felt tight. Unnatural. She unlocked the cottage door and led Mac inside. Her temporary home felt as grey as the weather outside but Julia didn't move to turn on any lights or heating. Neither did Mac.

This felt horribly awkward.

Mac looked as uncomfortable as Julia felt.

'Would you like a coffee or something?' she asked.

'Sure.' Mac followed her to the kitchenette. A tiny space that had always been made ridiculously small when he was sharing it with her. For weeks now, it had been a secret delight, the way she couldn't move in here without bumping into him or brushing past so close he would be obliged to catch her for an extra kiss or a cuddle.

It was the last thing she could cope with now. Why on earth had she offered coffee? She could hardly ask him to go and wait in the chilly sitting room and the only other room in the cottage was the bedroom. Oh…this was awkward.

Mac finally broke the silence.

'I'm sorry,' he said. 'I know you didn't want to see me today and you probably don't want to talk about this but something you said last night has been stuck in my head all day.'

Julia didn't say anything. She just waited, fiddling with the lid of the instant coffee jar, her fingers clumsy because they were only coming back to life slowly, a burning pain in them as the nerves warmed up. It was nothing on the pain lying in wait for her heart, though.

'That you'd been there and done that,' Mac continued. 'That you wouldn't believe anything I had to say. I need to know why.'

'Fair enough.' The jug had boiled but Julia ignored the waiting mugs. She turned to face Mac instead, backing up so she had the bench against her back in a futile bid for a sense of security.

'Three years ago,' she told him, 'I was engaged. To a man called Peter. We were very much in love and he knew my history. He knew I could never have children of my own and he convinced me that it didn't matter. That we could be childless or adopt or use a surrogate…that it wasn't an issue because he loved me and that was all that mattered. We planned our wedding, we dreamed about our future. We even bought a house.'

It was Mac's turn to be silent now. To wait. He stood there as still as a statue. Listening. Only his eyes moved. Scanning her face. Absorbing her words and analysing their significance.

'I believed him,' Julia continued. 'And why wouldn't I? He loved me and I loved him. I chose the wedding dress of my dreams. Everything was organised. All the grief I'd been through when I had to have the hysterectomy and knew I'd never have children was erased. I'd never been so happy.'

A muscle twitched in Mac's jaw as though he was gritting his teeth. 'And then?'

'Two weeks before the wedding date, Peter told me he was very sorry but he'd made a dreadful mistake.'

'What? In wanting to marry you?'

'In telling me that the fact I couldn't have children wasn't an issue. He'd discovered that having a baby with someone was actually quite a big deal. Becoming a father in a normal way. Making a family.'

'And it took until you were practically at the altar for him to come to this conclusion?' Mac sounded incredulous.

Julia looked away. 'I think the timing was more to do with the fact that someone else informed him he was going to *be* a father. A *real* father.'

Mac's snort was derisive. 'The scumbag was sleeping with someone else?'

'Obviously.'

'And he got her pregnant?'

Julia couldn't help smiling. 'And you got your degree with honours?'

Mac shook his head. Either he didn't remember his dig at Julia when she had been asking him about his siblings that day or he simply wasn't amused. 'I'm smarter than you are.'

Julia blinked. She had expected at least some sympathy for having been so badly treated. 'What's that supposed to mean?'

Mac turned away from her as though he had

no intention of answering the question but then he swung back to face her. 'You think you got dumped because you can't have children, yes?'

Julia's jaw dropped at the same time as her hackles rose. Surely Mac didn't think this was an appropriate time to come riding in on a white charger and sweep the issue into oblivion? Tell her that Peter was an idiot because it really didn't matter? The arrogance of the man!

'Actually,' she informed him, 'that was precisely why I got "dumped", as you so sensitively put it. Peter spelt it out. With a scarily similar lack of sensitivity.'

Mac shook his head again. 'Sorry, Jules. Seems to me you missed the point entirely.'

Julia's tone was pure ice. 'And the point is?'

'The fact that he was sleeping with someone else in the first place. You don't do that if you love someone enough to want to spend the rest of your life with them.'

You might if you think the person you're

going to marry isn't a 'real' woman. One that's capable of having a baby.

Not that Julia was going to say this aloud only to have it dismissed. She'd been nearly destroyed by the pain of what Peter had done. How could Mac belittle what she'd been through? Make her feel like she'd been stupid and had 'missed the point' or overreacted or something?

He didn't understand.

And why was he any different anyway? He'd never said *he* loved her.

He's shown you, her heart whispered. *Every time he's touched you and kissed you and smiled at you in that special way that makes you melt inside.*

That's just what you want to believe, her head countered. *'Just like you wanted to believe everything Peter said.*

Julia was torn. More than anything, she wanted to trust Mac but to do so was terrifying because she would be laying herself open to a pain she couldn't voluntarily submit to.

She couldn't do it.

She couldn't trust Mac. Something too powerful was holding her back.

Maybe she was wrong and she was being stupid and totally missing the point but it came down to the courage needed to trust and if she didn't have it, this was over. That was the crux of everything happening here, wasn't it? If you loved someone enough to overcome obstacles, you trusted them. It was a given.

Mac was staring at her.

Watching the way her head was overruling her heart.

Reading her mind.

'You don't trust me, do you?' He rubbed his forehead as though aware of the furrows of disbelief that had appeared.

'You don't trust me,' he repeated, his tone hollow now.

She didn't trust him.

Man, that was a kicker.

Mac had been prepared to do anything for this

woman but he was facing a wall that was so dauntingly solid he had no idea where to start trying to break it down.

He *loved* her, for God's sake. He could no more think of sleeping with someone else at this point in his life than... Good grief, he couldn't even think of something abhorrent enough to fill the gap.

She didn't trust him because she thought he was the same as the creep she'd been planning to marry. A man who clearly hadn't loved her and had used her inability to have children as an excuse for his disgusting behavior. His betrayal.

She had loved this Peter. She'd said so. She'd trusted him and had been betrayed and had her heart broken.

Fair enough. He got that.

If she loved *him*, she would trust him.

She didn't trust him. He'd made the accusation and she hadn't even tried to deny it.

She'd never said she loved him so why had he assumed she felt the same way he did?

Because he'd trusted her, that's why. He had felt it in every touch and every smile. Every moment of connection and underlying every silent conversation.

They were at an impasse here. Standing in this ridiculously small space with two mugs on the bench that were probably not going to have coffee in them any time soon.

The silence stretched on. When Julia broke it, her voice was tight.

'I'm not the only one who has a problem with trust,' she said.

'What the hell is that supposed to mean?'

'You've got things in your past you haven't trusted me enough to talk about.'

'You've never asked.'

'OK.' He recognised the tilt of Julia's chin. The same kind of determination he'd seen when she was doing something she probably shouldn't be doing. Like volunteering to dangle from a broken bridge or climb into an unstable train carriage. 'I'm asking now. What was it about the woman on that train? Who did she remind you of and why didn't you want to talk about it?'

Mac sucked in a breath. Did he have any hope of breaking through that wall or was this over? Was this the time to try even? But this was about trust and honesty and Julia had told him about the baggage she carried. She deserved the same from him.

'It was ten years ago,' he said slowly, 'and her name was Christine.'

'And she had long blonde hair?'

'Yes.' Mac breathed in. Carefully, as though the very air in this room was a source of pain. 'I thought I was in love with her. We hadn't known each other very long and I wasn't thinking about asking her to marry me but…she got pregnant.'

He'd known it would be rubbing salt into a wound. What he hadn't known was that the flash of pain on Julia's face would feel like he'd given her a physical blow.

'She didn't want the baby,' he continued woodenly. 'She never wanted to have children holding her back, stopping her doing what she wanted to do with her life. She saw it as an obstacle. Unimportant in its own right. And nothing I could do or say would change her mind because I wasn't important enough either. She had the abortion and told me about it in the email that also said she was leaving.'

There. He'd said it. Admitted the failure that had haunted him for all these years. Would it change anything? Make him more trustworthy because he'd been so honest?

'*You* wanted the baby, though, didn't you?' Julia asked softly.

Oh…God. Mac could never forget that moment when he'd been told about the baby. That clutching sensation around his heart. The shock that had become amazement at what had felt like a miracle. *His* baby. He was going to be a father. And hot on the heels of that had come the powerful urge to protect that baby. From anything. For ever.

Julia's gaze was fixed on his face. 'Of course you did,' she whispered. 'So don't try and tell me it doesn't matter, Mac. That we can get past this. We can't because I won't do that to you. End of story.'

This had to be the worst moment of his life. He wanted to tell her she was wrong. That ending this was wrong, but he couldn't find any words. Maybe there weren't any.

Maybe she was right.

That moment was imprinted on his heart for ever. The same kind of longing for his child—his own family—that he'd seen on Julia's face when she'd been holding Noni.

She understood. She didn't want to stand in the way of him finding that moment again.

Could he feel the same way about an adopted child? Or a childless marriage? The honest answer was that he didn't know. That there was an element of doubt. That there was a small but insistent voice suggesting that maybe Julia was right.

She must have seen that doubt in his face.

'Oh, Mac…' With a tiny sob, she held out

her arms and offered—or perhaps asked for—a hug.

Wordlessly, Mac gathered her close and held her.

Time stopped as they stood there. Holding each other tightly. Accepting that this was the end of the road.

'It's been good, hasn't it?' Julia asked finally. 'What we had?'

'The best,' Mac agreed. 'You're an amazing woman, Julia Bennett.'

She pulled away but she was smiling. 'Will that be in your report?'

'You can count on it.'

'Is it nearly finished?'

'Pretty close.'

Julia took another step back. 'Do you think you could maybe finish it by tomorrow? Say, drop it into the office at work by lunchtime?'

'Probably.' Mac had the distinct feeling he wasn't going to like where this conversation was leading. 'Why?'

'Because there's a flight leaving from Heathrow

tomorrow night. I could get a connection from Glasgow in the afternoon.'

'You've booked tickets? But you're not supposed to be leaving before next week.'

'I just made some enquiries. The tickets are on hold. I've got a few hours until I need to confirm whether I want them but I think I do, Mac. I think it's time to go home.'

She wanted this. She wanted to escape. Maybe it was for the best. How could he work with her now, knowing it was over? That he had no hope of winning the new future he'd begun to dream of? That perhaps she didn't even love him. Not the way he loved her, anyway.

Julia broke their eye contact. Made a movement with her hands that was a kind of plea.

'We knew this had to end, didn't we? If we make a clean cut now, it'll be easier. We'll be able to look back and remember the good bits. The best bits.'

Mac swallowed. He didn't trust himself to speak. He needed to get out of here.

So he gave a single nod and turned for the

door. Then he turned back, took two long steps and caught Julia in his arms again. Held her tightly.

'Mac?'

'What?' He didn't want to let her go. Not yet. Not ever.

'Don't come to the airport with me tomorrow. This is goodbye, OK?'

No, it wasn't OK. It would never be OK. Mac tightened his grip but somehow Julia slipped free. What was it he'd said about her that day? That she was a cross between a contortionist and a weightlifter?

She had her back to him now.

'Please go, Mac.' The words were so quiet they were almost a prayer. 'Please go now.'

CHAPTER TEN

IT WAS the longest journey in the world.

Nearly thirty hours from Glasgow, Scotland to Christchurch, New Zealand with only brief interludes of airport time in London and Singapore.

The physical journey was easy enough. All Julia had to do was put herself in the right place at the right time and she was taken to where she needed to go.

The emotional journey was a very different story.

How unfair was it that it didn't seem to help to know that her head had been right in stopping her heart from trusting Mac? It had been a fight to the death in that tiny kitchen between her head and her heart and when she'd heard the desolation in his voice when he'd accused her of not trusting him, it had been all she could do not to fall into his arms and deny it.

To tell him that she loved him. That she would trust him with her life and with her heart. For ever.

Her head had pulled out the big guns then and they had located their target unerringly.

She'd been shocked, hearing him talk about Christine. Seeing the pain in his face when he'd told her about the baby he'd tried and failed to save. *His* baby. One that he'd wanted so much it had been painful just seeing a pregnant woman who looked a bit like Christine *ten* years later.

If her head had needed any proof that she was courting disaster by allowing herself to take that leap of faith, she'd had it. In spades.

The only way to survive was to run and hide.

Thank goodness she'd made those phone calls to enquire about changing dates on the tickets she already had. Just in case.

And when she'd voiced her intention to leave,

she had seen Mac have the kind of heart/mind struggle she was only too familiar with. She saw the moment his head got the strongest position. The moment when doubt had clouded his eyes.

Yes. It had been a fight to the death. The heads had won and the hearts—her heart, anyway—felt like they were dying.

Anne was there to meet her at the airport. She took one look at Julia's face and gathered her sister into her arms.

'Oh, Jules. Poor baby. You're home now, I've got you. It'll be all right, you'll see.'

And it was, kind of. Anne did what she did so well, with unstinting love and support backed up by some stern advice. It helped being half a world away from Mac and back in a familiar place that he'd never entered.

By the time the jet-lag was over and she was back at work full time, Julia knew that while nothing would ever be the same again, she would survive. Somehow.

* * *

Nothing was the same.

Mac had been right on the money with that niggling fear that his work and his bed would feel empty when Julia had gone. His whole life seemed about as colourful as the relentlessly grey Scottish weather they were experiencing day after day.

He would get through it. He'd done it before.

Or had he?

Had he ever really got his head sorted after Christine? He had been so sure he had but now he was beginning to wonder if all he'd succeeded in doing had been to shove the whole emotional mess under a convenient mental rug. If it hadn't still been there, it couldn't have been uncovered so easily by that tragedy of the young woman on the train.

No hope of pushing things under any kind of cover this time. Julia seemed to be everywhere. Waiting to ambush him at every turn—just like she had when she'd waited for him in the car park that night.

When he'd kissed her.

The car park was bad enough with its associated memories. Arriving in the locker room
for a night shift on the day she'd flown out was
even more poignant. Julia had forgotten her
boots and there they were. Half a dozen sizes
smaller than any of the men's footwear, they
looked childlike and forlorn. Abandoned.

He could hear an echo of Julia's laughter in
here as well. Her voice with that determined
lilt.

'I might be smaller than you lot but I'm just
as tough, you'll see.'

She hadn't looked tough when she'd held her
arms out for that farewell hug.

Everybody was missing her.

'I wonder what Jules is doing,' Angus took to
musing at irritatingly frequent intervals. 'Has
she emailed yet to tell you why she had to go
home in such a rush?'

No. She hadn't emailed. Hadn't phoned. Hadn't
even sent for her boots.

A week passed. And another. Until Mac
couldn't stand the sight of those small boots any

longer. He parceled them up and made a call to the administrative offices to get Julia Bennett's home address. He posted them and then wondered if he would get any response to the cryptic note he had scrawled to go in the parcel.

Missing something?

If she'd missed the boots, she would have sent for them. If she missed him, she would have made contact. If Mac was going to get over this any time soon, he would stop thinking about her so often. The hurt at not being loved enough— *trusted* enough—would fade.

He went to visit his mother a week or so later. Jeannie MacCulloch took one look at her son's face and clicked her tongue.

'You let her get away, didn't you, Alan?'

'I couldn't stop her, Mum. She didn't want to stay.'

'Oh?' The look on her face was mischievous enough to remind him of the woman he'd lost. 'New Zealand is a bonny place, I've heard. I'm going there myself, you know. With Doreen.'

* * *

'You need a change,' Anne decreed. 'A fresh start.'

Julia sighed. 'I'm trying.'

'Did you go ahead with applying for that Urban Search and Rescue training?'

'Yes. It doesn't start for a couple of months, though.'

'Anything else interesting in the classifieds in that *Emergency Medicine* journal?'

'There's a road-based position here in Christchurch. A shift supervisor one that comes with a car to back up ambulance crews.'

'You don't sound overly enthusiastic.'

Julia suppressed another sigh. She wasn't. Not because it wouldn't be a great job but because it would be too similar to what she'd been doing with Mac when they hadn't been needed in the air, only she would be doing it by herself and the empty passenger seat in the front would contain his ghost.

'It comes with a ton of administrative re-sponsibilities.' Anne had done more than her share of listening to her heartache and providing support. It really was high time she pulled herself together. 'There's a bit of teaching involved as well. I quite like the idea of that.'

'Sounds good,' her sister agreed. 'Would it mean giving up the helicopter work completely?'

'Yeah.'

Anne was trying not to look relieved. 'You'd miss it, though, wouldn't you? The thrill of dangling on a line that looks like a thread of a spider's web while you save someone's life?'

'You know what? I think the thrill is fading. I'm almost over it.'

It was an ordeal, actually, climbing into a helicopter these days. Just the sound of the rotors was enough to make her look around to catch the echo of the kind of look Mac would have given her if he'd been there.

The kind that said she was safe. That he would look after her. That whatever they were going to face, they would be able to handle it because they were such a good team.

A parcel arrived the following week with

Mac's handwriting on it. Her name and address blurred instantly as her eyes filled with tears.

He'd sent her boots back. She hadn't missed them because she had plenty of footwear for work here.

It was Mac she was missing. Every minute of every hour of every day.

There was a letter in the same mail delivery. An invitation to be part of a team that was going to review the training programme for the emergency services. With her recent experience overseas and the glowing report that had come back with her, she would be able to make a valuable contribution. It would take her away from frontline work but the contract would only be for six months to a year.

The boots lay in their shredded brown paper on the table in front of her. The letter was in her hand. Julia had to blink away a fresh burst of moisture making her eyes sting to read it again.

Annie was right. She needed a fresh start and

here it was, being handed to her on a plate. A new challenge. A new life, hopefully.

An advertisement for a locum to cover Julia's position on the specialist emergency response team was put online within days and applications flooded in for the prestigious vacancy. From the wealth of applications, only six were shortlisted but the process would be thorough and each interview was expected to last at least an hour.

The selection committee consisted of the district manager of the ambulance service, a representative from the police and a clinical instructor who was one of the most experienced paramedics in the country. The reputation of the team was important to everyone and it would be better to be down a team member for a while than do damage by employing the wrong person.

At the last minute, Julia was asked to come in on one of her days off to sit in on the interviews.

'But I haven't even seen the C.V.'s,' she protested.

'I'd rather you didn't.' The district manager ushered her into the boardroom. 'I thought it would be valuable to get an unbiased opinion based on what you see and hear here today. This is your job they'll be doing. You're in the best position to assess qualities that may be relevant but don't appear in qualifications or get covered by the interview process even.'

So Julia sat in what had to be an intimidating row of a selection committee, on one side of the huge boardroom table. Applicants came in one by one and sat on the other side of the expanse of polished mahogany.

The first was an Australian. A confident man in his early thirties with great postgraduate qualifications and an impressive history of service in a helicopter squad.

'I've been on the choppers for years,' he told them. 'I'm just looking for a bit more. I compete in target shooting as a hobby and I do combat obstacle courses as exercise training. Working with the cops is an edge that appeals to me.'

'He seems well qualified,' the clinical instructor said to lead the discussion after the interview. 'Young, fit and keen. Ideal.'

'I think he should be looking to join the police force,' the district manager suggested. 'Or the army.'

Two candidates were local. One had excelled in academic achievements and road-based work but would need full helicopter training.

'Too expensive,' the district manager decreed. 'Can't justify it for a locum position.'

One candidate was female. A thirty-four-year-old paramedic from the north island.

'I want to challenge myself,' she admitted frankly during her interview. 'I've just completed my helicopter training and I'm excited by the opportunities this job could provide. I think I'd learn a lot and it would help me gain a permanent position further down the track.'

'She's got no idea how tough it can be,' was Julia's opinion, after asking searching questions during the interview. 'I think she needs more experience in general helicopter work. She's not ready for something like this.'

'We're getting through them,' the district manager reminded them. 'And so far there hasn't been one who's impressed us unanimously. That Aussie seems like the best bet.' He sounded weary. 'Guess we'd better see number five.'

The other members of this committee could empathise with the weary tone. Four hour-long interviews and a discussion after each one with only a short break for lunch. Julia's brain was beginning to feel fuzzy. The room was very warm so maybe she was getting dehydrated. She reached for the water jug to refill her glass, aware that the door was opening to admit the second to last applicant.

The jug was full and quite heavy so she had to watch what she was doing but that didn't prevent the hairs on the back of her neck lifting in an odd prickle of awareness. Maybe it was due to the sudden silence in the room as any shuffling or movement ceased. She had the sensation that everyone on her side of the table was sitting up and taking notice of the newcomer.

Already impressed.

And why wouldn't they be? Looking up as she gingerly set the water jug down, Julia was stunned to see the big, solid shape of Mac directly in front of her.

'Please…sit down,' the district manager invited. 'Alan MacCulloch, isn't it?'

'Mac will do just fine.'

Mac. He was here. Really here. Only a few feet away from her, but Julia couldn't move. These men around her were all well respected, top-of-their-field professionals. Should she step out of this interview, perhaps, because she was unable to be unbiased?

No. No way was she moving any further away from Mac. She was too stunned to make her legs work in any case.

'You have a very impressive C.V.,' the clinical instructor said, his tone slightly awed.

'Thank you.'

'And you've come from Glasgow, Scotland?' The police representative sounded amazed.

'Aye. I have.'

'That's a very long way to come for an interview for a position that's only temporary.'

'It is indeed.'

Julia cleared her throat. It had to be her turn to ask a question.

'Can…can I ask why you have?'

'Of course.' Mac smiled at her and Julia was aware of a melting sensation she'd been sure she would never feel again. It was one of *those* smiles. For her.

'I've been hearing what a bonny place New Zealand is,' Mac said. 'And I've had a yen to come and see for myself.'

Goodness, he was laying it on a bit thick, wasn't he? Even his accent seemed stronger than Julia remembered. It curled around her and seeped into her cells and warmed her whole body. Everybody else on the committee seemed to be lapping it up as well. Everybody had a smile on their face.

'I felt as though I'd reached the full potential my last position could provide,' Mac continued. He glanced at each committee member before making eye contact with Julia again. 'Like it had…gone past its "use-by" date, perhaps. I need something else and I'm ready to meet any new challenge.'

Julia's breath had caught in her throat. Had he known somehow that she was going to be sitting in on these interviews?

Surely not. But he knew where she lived, didn't he? He had posted her boots back.

The district manager's smile had faded. 'I have to say you're almost over-qualified for this position, Mac. We're a small operation compared to what you're used to. The time frame is also somewhat limited.'

'It's more than enough time,' Mac said. 'I'm confident I can find exactly what I need here. I'm confident I can provide exactly what *you* need.'

His words were being heard by the whole selection committee but it was Julia he was looking at. It was Julia he was really talking to.

Her mouth was as dry as the Sahara but there was no way she was about to reach for her water glass because she knew her hand would be visibly shaking.

The implications of this were slowly sinking in.

Mac was here. Because of *her.*

He had left his job.

They'd kept their relationship a secret so that it was no threat to the job he loved with such a passion. But he'd left it. His 'last position', he'd said. Had he resigned from the SERT to come to the opposite end of the earth simply to find her? On the off chance he could carry on with his career?

'I'm sure your skills would be welcome anywhere you chose to take them,' the district manager was saying now. 'You're clearly a valuable asset to any specialist emergency service.'

'Aye.' Mac's smile was modest. 'I've had a few offers. I need some time to choose where I want to be from now on. Where I'm needed the most.'

I need you, Julia wanted to whisper.

He'd said he was confident. He sounded confident. He said he could provide exactly what she needed.

What did he mean? What had changed?

God, it was so good to see him. Unbelievably good. Julia drew in a shaky breath and only then became aware of the silence. Of the fact that everyone seemed to be looking at her.

'So...' The district manager raised an eyebrow. '*Did* you have anything else you'd like to ask Mac, Julia?'

Oh...yes. Absolutely. But not here.

'No,' she said aloud. 'And I have to confess that I know Mac. I can tell you that this man's experience and reputation are unparalleled. If he wants to be here, for whatever reason, we would be privileged to have him.'

There were heartfelt murmurs of agreement from everyone else on the selection committee. It was a done deal but they had to be seen to be going through the process so the final applicant had to be interviewed.

And maybe that interview was the shortest one of the day but it was still far too long as far as Julia was concerned because it was long enough for Mac to have vanished by the time she could escape from the boardroom.

A wave of disappointment strong enough to make her falter and stand absolutely still, feeling utterly lost, fortunately lasted only the time it took to take a deep, steadying breath.

Mac had posted her boots back to her.

He knew where she lived and Julia knew exactly where he would be right now.

Waiting on her porch.

Because they needed to talk.

He had so much he wanted to say to Julia but there wasn't a single, coherent word in Mac's head when he saw her coming up the tidy brick pathway to where he was waiting on her porch.

The need to take her in his arms and hold

her close was so powerful it drove any other thoughts into oblivion because she was *running*. Discarding her bag heedlessly at the bottom of the steps. Flying up and into his arms with the force of a small tornado. Mac was actually knocked off balance and laughed aloud with the joy of it as he caught her.

And held her.

Laughter faded then. Julia's head was buried against his chest and he could feel her fierce need in the way her arms were reaching as far as they could around his body. In the tremor that came from muscles held so tightly. The catch in her breath that was a tiny sob.

He tilted his head so that it rested against the top of Julia's. He pressed his lips to her hair.

'It's all right, hinny. I'm here. I'm sorry it took so long.'

'What do you mean?' Julia's voice was muffled. 'What took so long?'

'For me to get here.'

'I wasn't expecting you.' Julia raised her head and Mac could see bewilderment in her face.

Tears in her eyes. 'You never called. Never wrote. The only thing I've had was the parcel with my boots in it and I thought…'

'What?' Mac gave her an encouraging squeeze.

'I thought that you were sending the boots back because you didn't want any reminders of me. That you thought my stupid boots were the only thing I could be missing.'

'Weren't they?'

Julia gave his chest a tiny thump. 'You know they weren't.'

Mac let his breath out in a satisfied sigh. 'I didn't know but now I do.' He kissed her forehead gently. 'And I have to admit I'm quite relieved.'

'You are?'

'Of course. Here I am, jobless and homeless and with everything I need for the rest of my life right here. I was a bit worried about what I'd do if you weren't pleased to see me.'

Julia was wriggling in his arms, looking around behind her.

'You've only got a backpack.'

'I travel light.'

'But you said you have everything you need for the rest of your life.'

'I do. I'm looking at it.' He could see the words hadn't connected. Julia was frowning.

'Have you really resigned from your job?'

'Aye.'

'But…you loved that job.'

'I can get a job I love anywhere. I wasn't lying in that interview when I said I had plenty of offers to choose from. What I can't get anywhere…' He turned Julia back to face him properly. To make sure she heard what he was saying. 'Is the woman I love.'

His voice cracked and Mac had to close his eyes for a heartbeat. The porch they were standing on in an ordinary little house in a Christchurch suburb vanished. He was on the beach on Iona now and the magic was strong. He opened his eyes to find Julia's gaze fixed on his face with a look of wonder. She could feel that magic too.

'I've missed you so much, Jules,' he said softly. 'I could have gone looking for someone else, like you suggested. Some woman who could give me ten children, but I would always feel like something was missing.' He had to swallow the lump in his throat and drag in a new breath. 'Part of my heart. My soul. The part I gave to you without understanding what was happening. The part I can only ever have back if you're by my side.' He tried—and failed—to smile. 'I want it back,' he whispered. 'I want *you*. I need you to trust this. To trust *me*.'

Her heart was filling to bursting point with something that felt like music.

All the time Mac had been holding her and telling her how much he loved her, Julia had been searching his face. Sinking into the depths of his eyes and trying to locate even the smallest hint of the doubt she'd seen there the day they'd said goodbye.

It wasn't there. Her head had to surrender to

her heart this time. There was no reason not to trust this.

'I *do* trust you, Mac,' she whispered back. 'And I love you. I've missed you *so* much but…I don't understand…'

Mac's hold on her was gentle now. He raised a hand and brushed tears from her cheeks but didn't say anything.

'I know how much you wanted that baby,' Julia said bravely. 'Even after so many years I could see how much you wanted it and how important it had been.'

'Aye…'

A shiver ran down Julia's spine at the quiet confirmation. Mac must have felt that shiver because he pulled her closer.

'I didn't understand either,' he told her. 'I hadn't thought about Christine or the baby for years. Not until I saw that woman on the train. Until you made me talk about her. I did a lot of thinking after you left, Jules, and the pieces finally came together. The whole picture.'

'What did you see?' The porch was an odd

place to be opening their hearts like this but it didn't occur to Julia to invite Mac inside her home just yet. There was magic happening here and it wasn't about to be broken.

'I thought I loved Christine,' Mac said, 'but what I actually fell in love with was that baby. The feeling like something had already been born that I could protect from anything and love for the rest of my life. It was…the feeling of family, I guess. Or something more important than myself. Something huge and warm and… more important than anything else could ever be.'

Julia could feel her whole body tensing. She'd been right. A baby…*his* baby…was that important. Something that had been ripped away from him and something she could never give him. So why was he here, holding her like this? How could she ever persuade him that he would regret giving up the chance to have that family?

'I was missing you so much I couldn't breathe

without it hurting,' Mac said then. 'And, finally, I understood.'

'Understood what?' Julia's words were a whisper of hope.

'That I don't need a baby. That I already had that feeling when I was with you. That urge to protect you from anything. So much love I know it will last for ever. I love you…' he smiled '…and that's all that matters.'

'But…'

Mac gave his head a tiny shake. 'We could have children,' he said. 'Our own with a surrogate or adopted. We could foster some or just borrow some from a friend for a weekend but it would be a bonus. We could have a puppy or a tank of goldfish or an elephant in the back yard if we wanted but we don't need any of that to be a family. We're the lucky ones.'

'We are?' She certainly felt lucky. Blessed beyond measure, but hearing Mac say these things was unbelievably wonderful. Maybe she'd heard them before but only with her ears. This time she could hear them with her heart and soul and she couldn't doubt a single syllable of them.

'Some people have to have children to make a family and then the kids grow up and leave home and they haven't got it any more. We've got it now. We'll still have it when we're old and grey.' His brow furrowed. 'If that's what you want, too?'

'Of course it is. I want to be with you, Mac. I want you by my side just as much as you want me by yours. And you're right.'

'About?'

'I hadn't thought it through, really. I thought about adopting children and that I could do it by myself if I had to and I would be able to love those kids as if I'd given birth to them myself. I could have made a family but it would never have stopped me missing you. I love you, Mac.'

'Will you marry me?'

'Yes.' Julia's joy bubbled out in laughter. 'Absolutely, yes.'

Mac's lips touched hers almost reverently and

those dark eyes Julia loved so much were suspiciously bright.

With love. For her.

'Thank you,' Julia breathed.

'What for?'

'For making a dream I didn't dare have any more come true.'

'We can make all our dreams come true if we do it together.'

Julia's smile wobbled. 'You know what?'

'What?'

'I actually believe that.'

Mac's brow creased thoughtfully. '*You* know what?'

'What?'

'Bed's a very good place for dreaming.'

Julia's laughter sounded like a joyous peal of bells. 'You'd better come inside then.'

EPILOGUE

'I'LL give you a moment to yourselves,' the doctor said. 'To let you make a final decision.'

He shut the door behind them and they were alone in this treatment room of the specialist private fertility clinic.

Julia's hand was being held tightly by that of her husband.

Her other hand was being held almost as tightly by her sister.

Anne lay on the bed, wearing a hospital gown, a sheet covering her bare legs.

Mac was eyeing the stirrups attached to the end of the bed. Julia followed his gaze and then looked back at her sister.

'Are you sure about this, Annie? It's not too late to change your mind.'

'I'm hardly about to take back my wedding

gift to you guys,' Anne said calmly. 'Not when it's taken this long to get you to accept it.'

It had taken a while but there had been good reasons for that.

The first month after Mac had arrived in New Zealand had passed in a blur of happiness and making plans. At the end of that month, they had been married in a simple ceremony on a beach.

Anne had been there, of course. She had loved Mac from their first meeting but the short engagement and low-key celebration of their commitment to each other had concerned her a little. When Julia had chosen a pretty sundress for the occasion, Anne had shaken her head.

'Are you sure this is all you want? I mean, you wanted to do the whole meringue thing last time.'

Julia had grinned. 'The dream wedding dress. Yeah…but this time I've got the dream man, Annie. I don't need anything else.'

'This is all happening so fast. I haven't even thought of what to get you for a wedding gift.'

'We don't need one. We love each other. We've got a week on a desert island for a honeymoon. We couldn't be happier, honestly.'

But she'd been wrong.

When they came back from their honeymoon, Anne had a gift waiting for them. A promise.

'I want to be a surrogate mother for you,' she said.

Julia's hand had found Mac's and they'd sat there, stunned by the incredible offer they were hearing.

'You'd be doing me a favour, really,' Anne said in the end. 'I don't want motherhood but if I missed the experience of childbirth I might regret it one day. And, hey, this way I'll be getting nieces and nephews and I can guarantee I'll always get an invitation to a family Christmas dinner.'

At first, both Julia and Mac had been too blown away to really consider the offer seriously.

And they were busy. Julia had loved her think-tank contract so much she'd accepted another one to set up a training programme in dealing with multi-casualty incidents.

Mac had been persuaded to accept a permanent position on the local specialist emergency response team with invitations to travel and train teams in other centres if he had the time and inclination.

They bought a house together, on a bush-clad hill overlooking a tiny private beach in a secluded harbour bay. They called the property Iona.

Jeannie MacCulloch came to visit them as she toured the country with her friend Doreen.

'You're a clever lad,' she told her son. 'I knew you'd see sense. But will you *ever* stop growing?'

Anne reminded them periodically that she wasn't getting any younger. 'I've got a sabbatical due half way through next year, so if you're ever going to accept this gift, this is the best possible time.' She had given them a knowing smile. 'There's some fine print you might have missed concerning a "use-by" date.'

They'd talked and talked about it.

Walking on what rapidly came to feel like their own little beach.

Holding each other at night after making love.

During telephone calls when one of them was out of town for a day or two. Separation that was only made tolerable by long, long conversations last thing in the day.

And, finally, they realised they were being offered a gift that was beyond price.

A bonus to their lives that they might not need but which would add to their happiness immeasurably.

Julia underwent treatment to stimulate her ovaries and then Mac held her hand while the egg collection procedure happened.

Mac did his part without a murmur of complaint at any indignities involved.

And here they were, nearly a year after their wedding, and a decision had to be made about how many embryos to implant in Anne's womb.

'Two's good,' the specialist had advised. 'If it's successful, twins are manageable and don't present too much of a risk of complications to the mother, and if one embryo fails to take, you've got back-up. Three is acceptable and gives you more chances for implantation but a riskier pregnancy if they all take.'

They agreed on two.

Mac went to call the doctor back to the room but paused at the door and turned. 'I can stay in the waiting room for the next bit if you prefer,' he told Anne.

Anne snorted. 'You're the father of these babies, Mac. You won't be in the waiting room for their birth so you may as well be here for the opening act.'

Mac grinned, clearly delighted. He came back a minute later with the doctor and the lab technician who carried a petri dish. A nurse also came in to uncover the trolley that had the sterile cannula and other equipment needed for this brief procedure.

Julia still held her sister's hand.

Mac stood just behind her, his hands resting lightly on her hips, holding her so that she was touching his whole body.

'Here we go then,' the doctor said cheerfully.

Anne Bennett thought about closing her eyes for this but looked up instead.

Julia was still holding her hand but she had tipped her head back to look up at Mac and he was looking down at her.

She saw the hopes and dreams of a young couple who were born to be parents in that glance.

She saw a love so solid and huge it brought tears to her eyes.

So she did close them.

And she made a silent plea that this part of their story would have a very happy ending.

MEDICAL™

Large Print

Titles for the next six months…

March

DATING THE MILLIONAIRE DOCTOR	Marion Lennox
ALESSANDRO AND THE CHEERY NANNY	Amy Andrews
VALENTINO'S PREGNANCY BOMBSHELL	Amy Andrews
A KNIGHT FOR NURSE HART	Laura Iding
A NURSE TO TAME THE PLAYBOY	Maggie Kingsley
VILLAGE MIDWIFE, BLUSHING BRIDE	Gill Sanderson

April

BACHELOR OF THE BABY WARD	Meredith Webber
FAIRYTALE ON THE CHILDREN'S WARD	Meredith Webber
PLAYBOY UNDER THE MISTLETOE	Joanna Neil
OFFICER, SURGEON…GENTLEMAN!	Janice Lynn
MIDWIFE IN THE FAMILY WAY	Fiona McArthur
THEIR MARRIAGE MIRACLE	Sue MacKay

May

DR ZINETTI'S SNOWKISSED BRIDE	Sarah Morgan
THE CHRISTMAS BABY BUMP	Lynne Marshall
CHRISTMAS IN BLUEBELL COVE	Abigail Gordon
THE VILLAGE NURSE'S HAPPY-EVER-AFTER	Abigail Gordon
THE MOST MAGICAL GIFT OF ALL	Fiona Lowe
CHRISTMAS MIRACLE: A FAMILY	Dianne Drake

MEDICAL™

Large Print

June

ST PIRAN'S: THE WEDDING OF THE YEAR — Caroline Anderson
ST PIRAN'S: RESCUING PREGNANT CINDERELLA — Carol Marinelli
A CHRISTMAS KNIGHT — Kate Hardy
THE NURSE WHO SAVED CHRISTMAS — Janice Lynn
THE MIDWIFE'S CHRISTMAS MIRACLE — Jennifer Taylor
THE DOCTOR'S SOCIETY SWEETHEART — Lucy Clark

July

SHEIKH, CHILDREN'S DOCTOR...HUSBAND — Meredith Webber
SIX-WEEK MARRIAGE MIRACLE — Jessica Matthews
RESCUED BY THE DREAMY DOC — Amy Andrews
NAVY OFFICER TO FAMILY MAN — Emily Forbes
ST PIRAN'S: ITALIAN SURGEON, FORBIDDEN BRIDE — Margaret McDonagh
THE BABY WHO STOLE THE DOCTOR'S HEART — Dianne Drake

August

CEDAR BLUFF'S MOST ELIGIBLE BACHELOR — Laura Iding
DOCTOR: DIAMOND IN THE ROUGH — Lucy Clark
BECOMING DR BELLINI'S BRIDE — Joanna Neil
MIDWIFE, MOTHER...ITALIAN'S WIFE — Fiona McArthur
ST PIRAN'S: DAREDEVIL, DOCTOR...DAD! — Anne Fraser
SINGLE DAD'S TRIPLE TROUBLE — Fiona Lowe